THE MAYFLOWER PROJECT

REMNANTS™

THE MAYFLOWER PROJECT

K.A. APPLEGATE

AN
APPLE
PAPERBACK

SCHOLASTIC INC.
New York Toronto London Auckland Sydney
Mexico City New Delhi Hong Kong Buenos Aires

No part of this publication may be reproduced in whole or in part, or stored in a retrieval system, or transmitted in any form or by any means, electronic, mechanical, photocopying, recording, or otherwise, without written permission of the publisher. For information regarding permission, write to Scholastic Inc., Attention: Permissions Department, 557 Broadway, New York, NY 10012.

ISBN 0-439-54409-2

12 11 10 9 8 7 6 5 4 3 2 1   3 4 5 6 7 8/0

Printed in the U.S.A.

For Michael and Jake

THE MAYFLOWER PROJECT

Hannibal's Carthaginian army had trapped the Romans under Varro in a place called Canae. Before the day was done the Romans would lose seventy-thousand men. Hannibal would lose less than six thousand. It was to become the very model of total destruction, total victory.

Annihilation.

It was the year 216 B.C.

On that same day, in that same year, a comet that had for millions of years traveled a long, cold, looping orbit around the sun slammed into a massive asteroid in orbit between Mars and Jupiter. The impact was so powerful it reduced the comet to dust. It knocked several smaller pieces from the asteroid and nudged them, along with the asteroid itself, from orbit.

The asteroid began a slow spiral that would eventually bring it to a fiery death in the sun.

Then, in the same year that Abraham Lincoln freed American slaves, the asteroid had a close encounter with Mars. It missed the planet by several hundred thousand miles but the gravity of Mars swung the asteroid into a faster, steeper descent.

The asteroid would never reach the sun. It had another stop to make.

CHAPTER ONE

"BANG."

Jobs was fourteen years old, and if this were the year 2010 and not 2011, and if this were not the state of California but, say, the state of Indiana or New York, he would not be driving a car. Alone. All alone.

The technology had come in 2009 with the Ford Libertad!, but laws were slow to change, slower than technology, and so far only Texas, Montana, and in this last year, California, had changed the laws to allow people as young as twelve to be alone in control, more or less, of an actual car.

Jobs's parents had bought the 2011 model Libertad! with two things in mind: the hideous commute from their home in Carmel northeast to Silicon Valley and Palo Alto, and their quiet, restless, gifted son.

The car was yellow. It produced 325 horsepower, which wasn't bad, though Jobs felt sure he could improve on that given time — the engine was computer-controlled, of course, and Jobs hadn't met a program he couldn't improve.

Still, it was his 325 horses. Three-hundred-twenty-five horses and all his on a Saturday mid-morning with the fog lifting off the Monterey peninsula and Highway One not too choked with tourists yet.

"Car: Turn on," Jobs said. The car read his finger-prints from the steering wheel and the engine started. It didn't make very much noise — it was a hybrid and since the batteries were fully charged, it was running on electric motors at the moment.

"My pleasure, sir," the car said in a noncommittal feminine voice, and added, "Operation will be in safe mode only." The car did not sound apologetic. The car sounded, if anything, just a bit doubtful. A hint of uptalk. Jobs could fix that: This was just the default voice. Five other preloaded voices were available: young male, young female, authoritative male, gender nonspecific, and the computer-simulated voice of beloved (and long-dead) actor James Dean — a tie-in to Ford's ad campaign.

Jobs said, "Car: Destination: South on Highway One, most direct route."

There was no uptalk in his voice, no caution or question. Jobs could talk to machines. People not so much, but machines, yes.

The car opened the garage door, backed down

the driveway, bumped out into the street, stopped, turned, and proceeded at the speed limit.

Jobs held his breath. It wasn't that he doubted the technology, no, he'd read about it, understood it, the sensors were all well-tested, the Global Positioning System was backed up with a fail-safe, the program had run millions of simulations before Ford ever put it into a car. No, he trusted the technology. It was his own emotions he mistrusted. That sense of getting away with something, of being unaccountably free, that's what made him hold his breath because surely, surely somehow it wasn't going to last.

And yet, the 325 horses stopped at the stop sign, and proceeded when safe, and took a left, and read the green light, and turned onto the highway, sped up and shifted gears and slipped neatly between a classic nineties-era Beetle and a semi pulling a Wal-Mart trailer.

Past a new golf course with sprinklers going, and all at once the Pacific Ocean was revealed. Buttery sunshine, robin's-egg skies, puffy clouds, a sailboat leaning far over, a warm, dry breeze coming in the open window, what was not to like? What was less than perfect in all this?

Jobs sat watching the scenery and watching the wheel turn, left, right, passing the Wal-Mart truck.

He wanted to drive. He wanted to hold the wheel. That's what was wrong. He wanted his feet on the pedals and his hands on the wheel. Could he bypass the security protocol?

"No," he told himself firmly. "No."

It would be wrong, and worse still, it would be the end of him driving till he was seventeen and could get a license.

"Plus, you don't know how to drive," he reminded himself.

Jobs was thin, even bony, average height, with blond hair that looked as if it had been largely ignored, which it had been. There was something puppyish about his body: hands and feet too big, legs too long, as if he had been put together in a hurry from components that didn't always match up.

He had too-prominent brown eyes that wore a distracted expression, as if they were usually turned inward and only occasionally startled into observing the outside world. His mouth's default expression was one of tentative near-smile. Like he was planning on smiling but kept forgetting to.

His birth name was Sebastian Andreeson. He'd kept that name until he was seven and read a biography of Steven Jobs. From that point on, he was Jobs.

"Car: Sound system on."

The stereo came on and defaulted to one of his dad's files: Green Day? Nirvana? One of those eternally unhappy bands from the nineties. Jobs couldn't keep track of them. At least it wasn't his mom's hip-hop.

"Car: Stereo: Search for opera. Neo, not classic."

A few second's delay and the full, rich sound of a tenor singing a popular aria from Molly Folly. It was one of those tunes you couldn't get away from: hooky, singable, but lyrically prosaic, to Jobs's ear at least.

He was on the point of trying for something different when he recalled: Didn't Cordelia love Molly Folly? Yes, he remembered, she did. He remembered that.

And the kiss.

The dance. The gym, decorated with streamers and balloons and flatscreens showing slo-mo montages of soaring flight videos. (The theme of the dance was All Can Soar!) He hadn't come to the dance with Cordelia. He'd wanted to, he'd thought about it, planned it, written several convincing speeches to be delivered to her in a very casual yet totally rehearsed kind of way.

But he hadn't asked her; she'd gone with her boyfriend. Jobs had been under the impression that she'd broken up with Hondo, but no, they were back together at the dance.

So Jobs had gone alone. Even his best friend, Mo'Steel, had a date. He had to be there, no choice, since he was the designated techie running the lights and flatscreens.

On his way to the boys' room he'd come across Cordelia crying in a gloomy hallway off the gym. He asked why she was crying. She told him. For the next straight hour.

Jobs was a good listener. He listened, without judging or interrupting or trying to exploit the situation to his advantage. (Hondo had done her wrong.) He listened and sympathized and offered a shoulder to cry on, despite the increasingly urgent need to pee.

And then, in a strange, tender moment, Cordelia kissed him. Not a brotherly, "thanks for listening" kiss on the cheek, but the real thing. Then, with a rueful smile, she walked away and Jobs ran for the boys' room.

He remembered every detail. He just wasn't sure what the details meant. Had he blown his big chance? Had she been all but begging him to become her boyfriend? Had he been just too noble for his own good? Or had he exaggerated the whole thing all out of proportion?

The car swept down the coastal highway, holding at about forty miles an hour, open road ahead now, but twisting and turning. It occurred to Jobs that he should just dial Cordelia up and stun and astound her with the fact that he, he alone, was in the car. No parents. He was the only (or at least one of the very few) ninth graders currently in possession of 325 horsepower.

He could call her up. He could swing by wherever she was and give her a ride. She might respond by saying, "Ever since that night, that lovely, perfect kiss, I've been fascinated by you, Jobs. I know you're like some uber-nerd, but I also sense that deep down inside you hide the soul of a poet. Now, please kiss me again."

Yep. That's what would happen.

The music stopped and Jobs realized he hadn't turned on the content filter. A news broadcast began and before he had a chance to instruct the car to go back to music, he heard something that froze the words unformed in his throat.

". . . denied the report and said that 'no credible evidence has yet been presented that Earth is directly imperiled.'"

And with that the broadcast turned to the next story, which involved stock prices.

"Car: Stereo: Previous story, give me the full file, on screen."

The Libertad! might not have been exactly perfect for a guy who wanted his hands on the wheel and his foot on the pedal, but it was perfect for someone who wanted to read.

The story appeared on screen, a compilation of news reports from *The New York Times* and CNN and WebboScreed.

The original story had come from Webbo-Screed. The story said that NASA had discovered an approaching asteroid roughly seventy-six miles long on an intercept course with Earth.

As he was reading the story a bug popped up to announce an update. This was a CNN story, a more credible source than WebboScreed.

"Car: Stereo: Play the bugged story. Video."

The screen showed a CNN anchor doing an intro to a piece reported with some skepticism by a field reporter standing out in a marsh near the Kennedy Space Center in Florida.

The reporter quoted sources as saying that one of the last of the aging shuttles was being outfitted to carry a sort of Noah's Ark of selected humans into space so that at least some humans would survive the impact of the rumored asteroid.

CNN went to some lengths to pooh-pooh its own story. There were endless reminders that this was totally unconfirmed, and in fact was being vigorously denied by NASA and the White House.

The reporter concluded by suggesting that he, personally, thought the story was baloney.

Jobs cleared the screen.

He took several deep, shaky breaths. Dangerous to automatically believe anything the media said. Unless it was confirmed, backed up, proven.

Or unless your mother had been weeping secretly for the last two weeks, giving you and your brother strange, faraway looks filled with muted horror and sadness.

And unless that mother was Professor Jennifer Andreeson, head of astrophysics at Stanford.

Asteroid. Seventy-six miles long. The asteroid that had eradicated the dinosaurs was what? Jobs searched his memory. Ten miles long?

It would be like shooting a bullet into a soft-boiled egg.

"Bang," Jobs said to the car.

He didn't know what to do or think. He could call his parents. He could call his little brother, Edward. He could call Cordelia and try to exploit the fact that the world was coming to an end. Or he could call his best friend, Mo'Steel, who would be absolutely no help at all.

"Link: Call Mo."

CHAPTER TWO

"YOU DON'T WANT TO BE IN A BODY CAST WHEN IT HAPPENS."

Mo'Steel had barely slept the night before. He'd barely spoken to anyone, which was unusual. He'd barely formed a coherent thought, which was not at all unusual. He was as excited as it was possible for him to be, and he was capable of becoming very excited.

He was not scared. Not what you'd call really scared. He was totally glandular, definitely hugely adrenalized, but not scared.

His friend Jobs had once tried to convince him that fear was the real motivation behind Mo'Steel's obsessive need for the newest, wildest, most idiotic, most dangerous thrill. But that was Jobs for you: He thought *way* too much. He wouldn't say anything for a week, then, when he finally did say something besides, "You gonna eat those fries?" what he said would be something disturbing.

Mo'Steel was hooked onto a semi-enclosed chairlift that moved about five times faster than the usual ski lift. But then this wasn't a ski lift. This wasn't skiing. No snow in sight at this altitude, though there was a nice snowcap higher up.

The lift was just a sort of hook, really, a bare little seat and a steel ring to hold him in place and a plastic bubble to trap oxygen and a bit of warmth.

His feet hung free. Fifty-foot-tall trees reached up practically to brush the wheels of Mo'Steel's skates as he skimmed along above them. The birds were all down there, flitting white and gray and russet shapes. He was above the birds.

He twisted in the lift to look back at distant Denver, smoggy and sprawled out at the foot of the mountains. He pitied those people down there. Pitied them because all they were doing was grinding along, stuck on slow, while he was on the edge of the ultimate.

He turned away from the city and peered down through the trees again. Here and there he saw sections of The Pipe. The Six Flags over Colorado Skateboggan was the official name, which was just pitiful. They should have known everyone would be calling it The Pipe. Capital T, capital P.

The Pipe was an eight-foot-diameter tube, all blast-glass, Teflon, and neon inside, dull brown-painted aluminum outside. It ran from near the top of Mount Cisco Systems all the way to the bottom: an eleven-thousand-foot drop. But not just a drop, oh no. The Pipe split into four intertwining, interlocking branches, zooming back and forth down the mountain's face, so that the eleven-thousand-twenty-foot vertical actually ended up being closer to twenty thousand linear feet.

Twenty thousand feet: three-point-eight miles, give or take. Maximum recorded speed? Seventy-eight miles per hour, compadre.

Fast as a car on the interstate, only with no car.

The peak, the launching point, was not far now. Mo'Steel was getting giddy and he wondered for a moment if the oxygen system was working right. Not much air way up here.

Not much air but plenty of wind. The little car rocked back and forth, not a bad ride all by itself. What if the cable broke? That could be woolly. Hard-core woolly.

He began to loosen himself up as well as he could. Shoulder roll, leg stretch, oh man, it was going to be supreme.

The voice of the chairlift informed him that he had one minute to blastoff and reminded him to check his equipment.

He slapped the helmet down on his head, made sure it was seated properly. He spun the little wheels set in the edge of his gloves. He kicked his skates together, testing the feel of them. Knee pads, on. Elbow pads, on.

Mo'Steel was not a big jock. He was never going to play professional basketball or football — he was too small for either. Not small small, just normal size, and normal size was death in pro sports.

He had broad shoulders and somewhat bowed legs and a concave belly. His face was defined by a wide, smiling mouth and eyes set too far apart for classic good looks. There was a reptilian quality to him, but a nice reptile: a happy lizard with quick movements and sudden grins and long brown hair that bounced every time he yelled. Which was fairly often since Mo'Steel's normal mode of conversation was a goofy, wild-eyed yell.

He was over the snow now, the almost year-round snow. The wind whipped up seriously, whistling over the mountain's peak, and pushed freezing tendrils through the chairlift's heat-glow.

They said the inside of The Pipe was warm. And

plenty of air, too. That was good because he didn't want to do this all numb and wheezing. The point was to feel.

The chair cleared a rock ledge and there it was, all at once: The Sink. There could be no other name for it, although the Six Flags people insisted on calling it the American Express Launch Point.

It was The Sink. Capital T, capital S.

It was sixty feet across, a rounded out, perfectly smooth dimple in the top of the mountain, carved into living rock. In the bottom of The Sink was a drain. That drain was the opening of The Pipe.

The chair rose, circled, jerked on its cable as it dropped lower.

Time to take the test.

"Lock and load," Mo'Steel said.

He opened the safety belt and dropped the three feet to the gently sloped upper sink. He could still chicken out if he wanted. He could skate out of The Sink and wait to catch the next downward chair.

Yeah. Right.

Mo'Steel had never bunnied out. He had broken five major bones — four of them so badly that they'd been replaced with either composites or regrown-bone-over-titanium. His left humerus, right clavicle, right tibia, and fibula were artificial.

He was proud of the damage. He'd traded his birth name of Romeo Gonzalez for the name Mo'Steel — either for Man Of Steel or More Steel, he couldn't quite recall which — right after the spectacularly gross (and painful) tibia-fibula break.

Breaking body parts was acceptable. Going all bunny rabbit was not.

Mo'Steel changed his angle of attack and dropped down, turned, caught a cool centrifugal, then cut down and all at once, no time for second thoughts now, he was in The Pipe.

The Pipe took it easy for the first three-hundred feet. Time to catch your breath, psych up, get ready. There were neon bands placed every fifty feet. The color of the neon changed depending on the slope. Here they glowed green. Later they would change to yellow. When you saw red bands flash by you were dropping nearly vertical.

And then, there were the big purple streamers that would warn you of approaching intersections, and the white strobes to let you know you were coming onto an airborne.

A lot to remember when your brain was screaming.

"Green, green, green," as Mo'Steel got used to The Pipe, got used to the diameter, the unmarred smoothness. He slalomed a little, riding up and down the sides. How fast would he have to be going before he could pull a three-sixty?

Then, all at once it was bye-bye, stomach, and he was blazing down through a blur of yellow.

"Aaaaahhhh! Aaaaahhhh!" he yelled, an expression of purest joy. "Aaaaahhhhh!"

His link rang in his ear.

What? He'd blocked his link, he had definitely blocked his link, and now he was crouched low, beating the air resistance, building speed, and the phone was still deedly-deedling in his ear.

Faster, faster, so fast he could go airborne with a fart. Red lights ahead!

"Yeah! Yeah! Yeah!"

So fast now the wind was vibrating his cheeks, stretching his lips into an oblong "O."

Going red! The red neon was a blur. A smear of blood-light all around him.

The link rang again. Distracting, to say the least, when the slightest wrong move would result in his sliding ignominiously down the entire remaining length of The Pipe. Oh, the humiliation!

Deedly-deedly.

"Argh! Link: Answer already!" he shouted in frustration. Purple streamer. Left or right? Left or right? He tried to remember the simulation he'd had to run through three times and master before he could be allowed to ride The Pipe.

Left. No, right!

A voice in his ear. "Mo, what's up?"

"Jobs? Aaaaaahhhhhh! Yeah! Yeah!"

"Mo, what are you doing?"

Left, left, left! A sudden, jerking, yellow-neon-three-gee-turn, then a sickening drop into all-red territory and man, he'd only thought he was going fast before. He was falling like a rock, gravity, Mother G had him, falling faster and faster, skates barely touching the tunnel.

"I'm riding The Pipe!" Mo'Steel yelled.

"What? Now?"

He pushed off ever so slightly, did a forward flip, and landed on his glove-wheels. Now he was rocketing along backward while standing (more or less) on his hands.

It was perhaps the most deeply satisfying moment of his life.

"Strobes!" Mo'Steel screamed giddily.

"Hey, this is kind of important, Mo."

Ahead there was a perfect circle of sunlight. Somersault. Upright and he was there before he could take a breath. There and all at once out of the pipe and flying through the air, shouting in glee, yelling, scared, wild, totally adrenal.

The gap was thirty feet. Thirty feet of open, pipe-less air. A flash of green and brown and a weirdly long, dream-slow view of blue sky.

The opening of the next segment of pipe was flared wide to allow for windage. Mo'Steel pulled his legs up, raised his toes, spread his arms out like wings and hit the flared lip perfectly.

"Jobs, you have got to do this! Aaaaahhhh! Aaaaahhhh!"

"Mo, listen to me, man: no more broken bones. Take it slow. Something is happening. Something big. You don't want to be in a body cast when it happens."

"Aaaaahhhhh! No, no, no yellow, no yellow, give me the red! Give me the red! Gimme RED! What's happening, Jobs? What big thing?"

"Mo, there's an asteroid going to hit Earth. I don't want to ruin your day, but it kind of looks like the world is going to end."

"Oh, that. Yeah, I knew that. My dad told me. Why do you think he paid for this trip? Is that it?"

A long pause. A peevish, dissatisfied silence. Then, "Yeah, Mo, that's it."

"Cool. Aaaaahhhhh! Later."

CHAPTER THREE

"IT WOULDN'T BE LIKE KILLING
IN A NORMAL WAY."

"Can't they blow it up?"

"No."

D-Caf thought about that for a moment. He trusted Mark, respected him. But at the same time he had always thought his brother lacked imagination. Mark was brilliant, no one argued with that, but he was not an imaginative person.

D-Caf said, "In this old movie I saw on TV, I forget the name, something about an asteroid, anyway, they blew it up. Most of it, anyway."

"It's too big, Hamster. If they were lucky maybe they'd knock a chunk off of it."

D-Caf bit his lip, then bit his thumbnail. "Don't call me Hamster. My name is D-Caf, everyone calls me that. You can call me Harlin if you can't handle D-Caf. Not Hamster."

"Whatever." Mark returned his gaze to the monitor, gazing intently, working, worrying an idea, tapping fitfully at the keys, occasionally muttering a simple spoken command.

D-Caf watched with what minimal patience he could summon. His brother had just announced the end of the world, and he seemed almost uninterested, distracted by the streaming number series on the monitor.

"Aren't they at least going to try?" D-Caf pressed. "I mean, in this old movie they landed on the comet, I mean I think maybe it was a comet, and they were drilling holes down into it and putting nuclear bombs and —"

"Let it go, Hamster. Just let it go, all right?" Mark yelled. He slammed his hands down together on the desktop, sending a souvenir pencil holder from Ocean City crashing to the floor. He leaned over and picked it up, put the pencils back in, and returned the cup to its place.

"Look," Mark said, "it's too big, it's too fast, it's too close. It's about four days away. If you dug a hole right to the center of it and piled every bomb on Earth in there all you'd do is crack it in half and both halves would hit Earth. Or maybe you'd melt some of it, and then we'd get hit by two great big rocks plus a few million cubic yards of molten rock and maybe some nickel and iron. You got the picture?

Last big rock that hit Earth drilled a hole about a mile deep and left a crater almost a mile across. You know how big that rock was? One-hundred-fifty feet. Not miles, feet. So guess what? The Rock is coming, the Rock is going to hit, and it's going to be like swinging a sledgehammer into a watermelon."

Mark spun back to his monitor, mad at himself for blowing up at his little brother, mad at D-Caf for making him blow up. He was more than just a big brother. He was all D-Caf had for family. Their parents had died ten years earlier when Mark was fifteen and Harlin was five. Under most circumstances the brothers would have been sent to foster homes. But Mark Melman was a resourceful kid. A prodigy in the arcane world of data flow mechanics. He was already employed by a major e-tailer while still in school, and he was able to use his income and his skill to evade the Maryland child protective services and keep his brother with him.

Once he turned eighteen he sought and was granted legal custody. By then Mark Melman was employed by Oono Systems Inc., which, among other things, held major contracts with NASA.

He had raised his little brother, doing a good job, mostly. But there had always been stresses and resentments. Mark hadn't had much of a childhood himself and the weight of parenting had made him short-tempered, impatient.

And D-Caf was honest enough about himself to know that he had never been an easy kid to handle. He was a daydreamer, a spacer, a person for whom ordinary life seemed dark and dull and slightly threatening. He spent his days reading, playing by himself, wandering away on long walks by the bay, watching the sailboats, forgetting homework, times, dates, duties. He would gladly have spent from sunrise to long after sunset with his face buried in a book, living a vicarious life.

When he was around people, in school, at church, at the summer camp his brother forced him to attend each year, he switched personalities entirely, becoming hyper, chatty, nervous, like someone on his tenth cup of coffee. (Hence the name D-Caf.) He made bad jokes. Too many bad jokes. People made him tense, and tension made him jumpy. The presence of other people had a sort of toxic effect on D-Caf, like they were a drug that altered his sense of himself, turning him into someone that he himself could not stand.

He was getting that way now, he could feel it, reacting to Mark's tersely delivered, shattering news. His leg was bouncing. He was rocking back and forth.

"They can't just sit around, though. I mean, they're trying something, right? I mean, all the technology we have, all the scientists and all."

Mark snorted derisively. "Yeah. They're trying something all right. They're calling it *Mayflower*. That's fairly pathetic. *Mayflower?* They had two weeks' notice. What do you think they're going to do in two weeks, build themselves a brand-new ship? They're hauling some tired old shuttle out of mothballs, tacking on every half-tested bit of quack technology they can find — I mean, solar sails, hibernation, anything lying around in somebody's lab. They're gonna tack it all onto this shuttle, load it up with people, and shoot them off into space."

"And they're going to blow up the asteroid?"

"No, Hamster, they're going to go floating off through space like some lost lifeboat. That's the big plan. That's it. That's all they've got."

Mark's voice dripped contempt. But then contempt was Mark's default tone. "Eighty, ninety people, whoever they can round up on no notice. For about ten seconds the NASA brass considered assembling some neat cross-section of humanity, geniuses of every type, every race and whatnot, then they realized, oops! They had no time for all that. NASA started handing out tickets to the people they needed, the people they owed favors to, the people who might screw up the plan if they weren't taken care of. And they're going to send those poor fools floating off through space, more or less aimed at a star they think might have a livable planet, which they might reach in a century or two, by which point they'll be freeze-dried, radioactive, as full of holes as Swiss cheese, and oh, by the way, dead."

D-Caf and his brother were like a before and after picture. The younger brother was fighting a weight problem, the older, Mark, looked like a guy who might not have exactly won that battle but had at least avoided losing it.

D-Caf had dark hair, dark eyes, teeth that would need correcting. He was already as tall as Mark and on his way to being taller. But he concealed this advantage by his habit of walking a little stooped forward. He had been tested in the usual ways and was, in fact, a bit more intelligent than Mark. But this was another advantage D-Caf could never exploit. Mark was his parent and his brother, and their relationship depended on an assumption of superiority for Mark. D-Caf had no interest in challenging the one real relationship he had.

D-Caf considered Mark's statement, the way he delivered it, the sense of things being left unsaid. He was practically vibrating, forehead frowning and re-leasing, frowning and releasing, trying to resist the cascade of tension-agitation.

"Can we go?" D-Caf asked. "Can we go on the shuttle?"

"Didn't you hear what I just told you?"

"Yeah. But you kind of look on the negative side of stuff, Mark."

To D-Caf's surprise, his brother barked out a genuine laugh. "Yeah, I do, huh? But, Ham — but brother, this isn't about positive or negative. The Rock hits, that's it. I wasn't going to tell you. I was just going to make it all good for you: movies every night, all the junk food you want, whatever you wanted because what does it matter anymore, right? But even if you are annoying sometimes, you're a very smart kid, and I've never lied to you yet."

D-Caf looked hard at his brother's face. There was something more, something he wasn't telling. D-Caf had the gift of knowing people's emotions, understanding. Empathy. He felt some hesitation, some indecision from his brother.

He waited, and stared, and said nothing, and at last Mark sighed and hung his head. "We can't go on the *Mayflower* because we're not a regular, stable family. That's what they're looking for. They're rounding up NASA people and NASA contractors, and yeah, maybe that's me, but only intact families. Anyway, the whole Mayflower Project is a stupid waste of time. But I guess there's a small but measurable chance it will succeed, and no chance with anything else." He sucked in a deep breath and looked hard at his brother. "So, look, if you want to, we're going."

"How?"

Mark leaned forward. He twined his fingers, twisting them almost painfully. "Everyone's doomed, brother. Everyone's death warrant is signed, sealed, and waiting to be delivered. So killing . . . I mean, it wouldn't be like killing in a normal way. And I still have Dad's old gun."

D-Caf blinked. He knew his brother didn't believe his own words, but he also knew he was very serious.

"The crew of the shuttle, just two guys, they have to deploy these experimental solar sails after they're in orbit, well into the flight. There's a space that connects the flight deck to the pod, the *Mayflower* capsule, whatever you want to call it. They have two hibernation berths there for the crew, just above the rest of the berths. They'll come back there after they deploy the sails and carry out their final burn. That's where we'll be, Hamster. That'll be our place. We'll be waiting."

CHAPTER FOUR

"YOU UP FOR SOMETHING STUPID AND DANGEROUS?"

A weird day had passed since Jobs had guessed the truth from the much-dismissed news story. A day when he had gone to school, done his homework, followed his usual routine.

His parents had said nothing. But for the last twenty-four hours the air in their home had been electric with unspoken fears. Conversation was stilted. His mother's eyes were rimmed with red. His father withdrew into a shell of silence, reading the paper for too long without turning a page, staring at nothing, squeezing his wife's hand too often.

But the next day, things changed. The atmosphere was just as charged, but Jobs guessed that whatever consideration had imposed the delay, the time had come at last.

Jobs's parents were waiting for him when he got home from school. They asked him to stay home.

That night, after a family dinner, after Edward had been freed to go play in the family room, they made it official: It was real.

"It will be devastating. I mean, you can do the math, son," his mother said.

"There's this escape plan. They call it *Mayflower*. It's an old shuttle loaded up with new technology. Hibernation," his dad added helpfully.

"I've read about the hibernation technology," Jobs said. "They tested it on baboons. Sixty-two percent of the baboons survived. That means thirty-eight percent died. And that was a short-term test: twelve hours in hibernation."

"That's just what's been declassified," his mother reassured him.

But his dad gave him one of the secret looks they sometimes shared. Jobs and his father had an agreement, a sort of truce that papered over the fundamental differences between them: They didn't lie to each other. Jobs nodded slowly: message received. His mom was trying to soften reality.

It was a lot to absorb. One thing to deduce, based on sketchy, not-entirely-serious news reports that the world was coming to an end. A whole different thing to have your parents lay it out.

His father said, "The thing is, kid, they'll come for

us sometime in the next day or so. In the meantime, we're being watched. All communications in and out of the house are being monitored. Same with the cars, with your link. You can't talk to anyone about this."

"I called Mo yesterday after that news story ran. He was in Colorado. He already knew."

"And you got the call to go through?" His mother frowned. "Idiots! On an open link and they didn't block it? You encrypted at least?"

Jobs nodded. "Of course, Mom. Mo and I have our own cryp."

"Thank God for that at least. This can't get out. The shuttle only carries so many people, you know, and almost all the spots are spoken for. There would be panic."

"The story was on CNN," Jobs said.

His father waved a dismissive hand. "That's a deliberate leak. They set it up so they can knock it down. Makes the newsies cautious about reporting anything else on it till they're dead sure." He winced. "Bad choice of words."

Jobs went to his room. He contacted Mo'Steel on his link. The call did not go through. Dead air. He e-mailed. E-mail returned, unreceived. Weird.

He sat there, staring at the glowing screen of his

main monitor. How could he punch through? He could tack an e-mail onto a virus, piggyback it onto a simple request for a movie.

He had a virus he'd used before, a benign, harmless, nearly invisible virus created only as a test. He called it up, bundled it into a standard request to view a movie. What movie? He thought for a moment. *Lord of the Rings, Part III.*

He punched in the request.

Request denied: virus detected.

And then, an instant message from Watcher 27@DSA. The IM said, "Nice try, kid."

Jobs didn't answer. He pulled his hands away from the keyboard.

DSA: Data Security Agency. He was being actively monitored by the DSA. Jobs had often considered a career that would begin with a couple of years at DSA.

He couldn't reach Mo'Steel. That was clear. Of course, he wasn't really interested in reaching Mo. Mo was already in the know, Mo could take care of himself.

Cordelia was a different matter.

What would I even say? Jobs wondered. *You barely know me, but the world is ending and maybe I could get you on some doomed shuttle to nowhere?*

A silly, romantic gesture, he knew. Grandiose. Melodramatic. Ludicrous.

But the need to do it, to try, to make the grand, silly, romantic gesture, those feelings were real. He couldn't just do nothing. He couldn't just write off the human race, so long, Earth, so long, Homo sapiens. So long to the kiss.

He noted with some surprise that he felt like throwing up. He was sweating. His hands were shaking. It disturbed him being this disturbed.

He tried to take deep breaths, tried to calm himself down, impossible to do any good thinking when you were this upset. Deep breath. Deep breath.

"Calm down?!" he demanded, outraged at himself. "Calm down? Everyone is going to die, calm down?!"

Sudden thought: *Had they bugged his room? Were they watching him even now, watching, listening, and getting readouts on his pulse and respiration and brain waves?*

He shot a look around his room. Pointless, of course: The sensors the FBI had access to were too small to be detected without the right equipment. Yes, of course they were watching, of course.

How to play it out? They'd seen him try to contact Mo. Seen him from both sides of the keyboard. Still, their resources must be limited.

He got up and went to the bathroom. He turned on the shower, hot and hotter. He cranked on the air-conditioning and closed the fan vent. Steam.

Lots of steam, that was the trick. Wet heat would confuse the sensors, the steam would cloud the tiny lens.

He let the steam build up, and, very self-consciously, took off his clothes. He was going to take a shower. A perfectly normal thing to do.

When the steam was dense enough he slipped back into his clammy clothing, opened the bathroom window, slid out, hung by his fingers, sucked it up, and dropped the eight feet to the ground.

He rolled, stood up, looked around the dark backyard. In a crouch he ran for the back fence. A jump, a grab, a painful roll across the top.

"Ouch. Ow. How does Mo do this kind of stuff?"

He was in the Ludmillas' yard. They didn't own a dog, fortunately.

He ran across their yard, cut left, and climbed their shorter fence, landing in the alleyway. It was just a block to Mo'Steel's house. Mo would probably be in the backyard: His family had a pool, and it was a warm night.

Jobs ran full speed. They'd know he was gone by now.

He reached the fence around Mo'Steel's back-yard and saw his friend fly through the air, soar above the fence into view, then fall with a huge splash.

He jumped, used the fence to do a pull-up, stuck his head over, and saw Mo'Steel spitting water. He was trying to drag a stainless steel mountain bike up out of the shallow end. Mo had rigged a ramp to drop from the backyard swing set, onto the diving board. He was convinced that he could get his bike to jump the pool lengthwise, if only he could build a high-enough ramp.

"Mo!"

"T'sup, Duck?"

"You up for something stupid and dangerous?"

Mo'Steel grinned like a four-year-old offered a lollipop. "Who, me?"

CHAPTER FIVE

"WELL, YOU KNOW WHAT HAPPENED TO THE DINOSAURS, RIGHT?"

In his dream Billy Weir flew across a great emptiness. An emptiness so vast, so hollow, so ringingly empty, so utterly without form or characteristic, there seemed no possibility of an ending. It was emptiness, blankness, a hole not in the ground but in the fabric of time and space itself.

He flew, immobile. He flew and his body was changed, somehow.

At times as he flew through the void he recalled the orphanage in Chernokozovo, Chechnya. He tasted the mold on the bread. He smelled the urine reek from the latrine, the reek that permeated the whole room. The cold, always cold, paint peeling from damp stone walls.

Other times he was in his room, in the house in Austin, Texas, the shockingly large, impossibly clean, opulent house where they fed him barbecue and corn and green salad.

Billy Weir. Not a taken name, a given name. He had been born Ruslan. That was his first name. No one ever told him his last name; it wouldn't have been safe: His father was a guerrilla fighter and the Russians were not above using him to hurt his father.

When the Weirs adopted him at age three he became William Weir III. At school, Billy Weird.

His dream drifted to school. He was teased but not harshly. Liked but not much. Accepted without enthusiasm. He wasn't even weird, except for the dreams, and no one knew about them. No one knew that in his dreams he remembered everything, everything, things he couldn't possibly remember: being a newborn baby, being three months old, and the murder of his mother by scared-drunk Russian troops. Things no one remembered but Billy.

And then there were the dreams, just as real, but that seemed to be about events that had not yet unfolded. Those dreams, those places all lay across that great, horrible void.

He saw a world of brilliant copper-colored ocean and pale pink skies and a ragged group hoisting sails on tall masts to catch the wind. A wild kid was hanging from the ropes yelling.

He saw mountains like knife edges. He saw great, buoyant beasts as big as blimps that bounded across a landscape of waving yellow grass.

He saw other creatures, creatures without faces, without arms or legs. Was he, himself, one of them?

But all that was far, far away. And what he saw most was the Rock. He dreamed of it, spinning, silent, no rush of air, no swoosh, no sense of its enormous speed. Just a monstrous rock, as big as a whole mountain chain, hills and pockmark craters and strange, fanciful extrusions.

He saw the Rock. He saw that his father, his adopted father, knew it was coming. The Rock would chase Billy Weir away to yet another home, another country. The Rock would make him an orphan again.

There was no resisting the dreams. When the dreams came they spoke the truth as it had been, as it would be.

He woke. He'd fallen asleep on the couch watching football. It was only about nine o'clock.

Sadness washed over him. Sadness had always been with him. Always from the start, from birth in a hollowed-out stone house, roof blasted away. He had come into the world without a cry, they thought he was dead, they almost hoped he was dead because what life could he ever have?

His mother, his true mother, had cried as she nursed him for the first time. And many, many times more as she carried him from place to place, always harried by the distant and not-so-distant sounds of artillery, the sharp crack of rifle fire.

He woke and the sadness was all over him, all through him, the dream still fresh in his mind. His father and mother were coming.

They were in the kitchen doorway. "Son, did you wake up?"

His mom and dad, Jessica and Big Bill Weir, as he was known, all went into the kitchen. Big Bill was just home late from work: a suit, a tie, polished alligator cowboy boots. His mom was in her robe.

"Sorry to make you miss the game, son," Big Bill said. "But we got the okay, so, anyway, I had to talk to you."

"It's fine," Billy said.

His dad looked at him, lips pursed, thoughtful, perplexed. Billy knew his dad had always done his best to treat Billy like a natural son. But despite those best efforts there seemed to be immutable differences between them. They didn't fight. They didn't argue. Billy was a good kid, respectful, proper, rarely headstrong. And, he knew, that was part of the problem, because Big Bill was known as a Holy Terror, a wild man of the high-technology world. He had loved it when *Business Week* called him a maverick.

Billy was not a maverick. Not a Texas-style maverick, anyway. He was small, for one thing. He had pale skin that never seemed to tan. He had deep, deep black eyes and unruly black hair. He was a good-looking kid in his own way, but he wasn't Big Bill.

And yet, Billy knew, his dad admired him. When he was twelve Billy had been in a very one-sided fight: An older kid, twice Billy's size, had beat him up in retaliation for Big Bill's firing his father. The older kid had broken his nose, kicked him so severely he peed blood for a day. Billy refused to take off from school. He refused to be driven to school to avoid walking by the bully's house. And when the bully's father brought his son over to make a contrite and frightened apology, Billy just listened, said nothing, showed neither fear nor resentment.

Big Bill didn't say much at the time. But the next day, for the first time, he brought Billy to work, to the company he owned. "Figure it's time for you to start finding out what our family does for a living. Meet some of our people, see our company."

The "our" was subtly underlined.

Now Big Bill was watching his son closely as he delivered the news. "Son, I have something to tell you. In the morning some men are coming. FBI agents, to tell it true. They're going to pack us up and take us away."

"Why?"

"Something terrible is about to happen. You know how you used to like to play with dinosaurs when you were little? You could name them all, I think. *Brachiosaurus,* all those. Well, you know what happened to the dinosaurs, right?"

"Yes, sir."

"A couple weeks ago they found a big old asteroid and it's coming this way. And there's no way to stop it. So, well, we're going to try hard not to be here when it hits. There's a mission. They're going to use the solar sails we've been developing, what do you think of that, eh? Of course, I have to tell it true: It's all one heck of a long shot."

"It will work," Billy said.

Big Bill smiled. To his wife he said, "The kid can take it."

Billy did not return the smile. He could feel himself rising up, floating, hanging now very, very near the edge of the endless void.

So close now, that nothingness. Normal time, this whole world already seemed shriveled and insignificant beside so much emptiness.

"Can we bring anything with us?"

His mother spoke for the first time. "Not very much, sweetheart. One or two small things, maybe, they said. It's all . . ." She looked around at the gleaming kitchen. There were tears in her eyes.

"I'll go pack," Billy said.

(CHAPTER SIX)

"IT'S JUST NOT HERO TIME."

"How are you going to get them to let Cordelia come along?" Mo'Steel asked.

"Blackmail," Jobs said.

"Cool."

They were trotting along the alley, Jobs dressed in still-damp clothes, Mo in a bathing suit, barefoot.

"I'm going to threaten to go straight to the media," Jobs panted.

"When we get to Cordelia's house I'll use her link to creep my mom's computer at work. They won't be monitoring Cordelia's link. I'll creep my mom's files — I know her codes. I'll upload them into half a dozen time-release files spread all over the Web. If they don't give me what I want, my mom's files on the Rock will be everywhere in a hurry."

Mo'Steel nodded. As usual, Jobs had a plan. Jobs

always had a plan. But discussions of computers tended to cause Mo'Steel's mind to wander, and after ascertaining that Jobs had some kind of plan, he lost interest in the details.

He did not lose interest in what was happening around him. Specifically the two dark sedans that roared down the street, crossing the alleyway. There was a screech of brakes and the whirring sound of a car thrown into reverse.

"Are we being chased?" Mo'Steel asked.

"Yeah. Maybe."

"Woolly. Come on, Duck. Follow me."

Mo'Steel leaped onto a trash bin, balanced precariously, stepped onto the top rail of a high fence, balanced there for a split second and jumped onto the sloped roof of a garage.

Jobs did his best to follow. Fortunately Mo'Steel had a pretty good idea of his friend's physical coordination and he had a strong hand ready to grab Jobs's flailing arm and pull him up.

A sedan came down the alley. Someone inside was shining a powerful flashlight into dark corners. The light swept just beneath Jobs's dangling legs.

On the garage roof Jobs gasped, "Thanks, Mo. I would have made it, you know."

"Sure you would, Duck. No question," Mo'Steel answered. "Come on."

"Let's get down."

"Down? Why would we get down? Look: There's a tree."

He led the way across the garage roof, into the low-drooping branches of an ancient elm. They threaded through the branches, up, down, squeeze. Across the fence to drop into the next yard.

Then it was across the yard, climb the rose trellis to the roof of the house, over to the far side, out onto that attached garage, a jump onto an RV parked in the driveway, and a heart-stopping leap that took them over a picket fence.

Jobs landed and plowed forward. Mo'Steel grabbed his arm and yanked him back. "Careful of the roses, compadre. Thorns and all. Besides, the old lady who lives here is nice."

A quick look left and right and they bolted across the street. Then through a gate and smack into a very large dog.

"*Rrrrr.*"

"Mo!"

"He's on a chain!"

"It's a long chain!"

With a guttural roar the dog charged.

"Jump him!" Mo'Steel yelled and leaped straight up as the dog passed beneath him. The animal hit Jobs head-on, bowling-balled him down and stood snarling on his chest.

"Aaahhh!" Jobs yelled.

Mo'Steel grabbed the chain, yanked the animal off Jobs, dragged the chain fast, and looped it around a cast-iron lawn chair.

"Come on, Duck, what are you waiting for?"

Jobs jumped up, cursing under his breath, and ran past the frantic, air-snapping beast.

Two more fences, one more roof, and a lung-crushing trip over a swing set and they were in Cordelia's backyard.

"Yesterday I do The Pipe. Now I'm Spider-Man," Mo'Steel exulted. "It's been a sweet couple of days."

Jobs gritted his teeth and narrowed his eyes. "Yeah, it's been a party, Mo. You are deeply disturbed."

Mo'Steel nodded in agreement. He was aware that he was different. He liked the difference.

They stood gazing up at Cordelia's window. No light showed.

"How do you know that's her room?" Mo'Steel asked.

"I know where her room is."

"You been up there?" Mo'Steel shot Jobs an incredulous look. Then he laughed. "Just in your head, right? L-o-o-o-ve. Makes a boy go crazy."

"How do I get up there?" Jobs wondered aloud.

Mo'Steel frowned. "Go around to the front door and knock. You can't be climbing in some girl's window."

"What? Hey, those guys could be waiting for me around front."

"Yeah, and your babe could be changing clothes or picking her nose or whatever, Duck. You have to treat fems with respect, you can't just be sticking your head in her window. Who raised you? Monkeys?"

"Mo, it's kind of an emergency. Now, how do I get up there?"

Mo'Steel looked around. He spied a picnic table. "Come on."

They manhandled the heavy table into place and leaned it up against the siding. Then Mo'Steel piled a wooden chair atop the upturned table.

"Climb on up: easy as a ladder."

Jobs began the ascent. *Not as easy as a ladder,* Jobs thought, *but not impossible, either.* But now he had some time to consider the next step: actually confronting Cordelia.

What on Earth was he going to say? Hi, it's me,

Jobs, I wanted to stop by and let you know the world is coming to an end but I think I can use blackmail to get you a berth on a probably doomed shuttle to nowhere?

He looked down at Mo'Steel. Too late to back out now. Not after all they'd gone through. Besides, maybe, maybe she'd believe him, and maybe she'd go along with his plan.

"I'm an idiot," Jobs muttered as he stood up to his full height and stretched to slide the window upward. A breeze carried delicate white curtains out, along with the scent of perfume: Bulgari Pink. He'd made it his business to find out.

"Cordelia," he whispered. "Don't be afraid. It's . . . it's Jobs."

He pulled himself up as well as he could. No answer. He sensed the emptiness of the room.

He climbed in, feeling that he was very definitely doing something wrong. But he had to do it anyway.

It was a girl's room, definitely a girl's room. There were stuffed animals, that was a dead giveaway. But she wasn't a Jane at least. No frills, no retro-Vic tea set or gold-framed pic of Jane Austen, the patron saint of the Jane clique, or the Skirts as they were sometimes called. He'd worried about that, early on, what with her name being Cordelia. No way a Jane and a Techie ever got together. But it had turned out Cordelia was her given name, so blame her parents.

Anyway, this room was a girl's room, but a cool girl. She had a pair of screens doing slow-dissolves of pix. Pix she must have taken herself, of places Jobs recognized, hangouts, parts of the school, people he knew. Also landscapes, sunsets (*kind of a cliché choice,* he thought), and seascapes.

He stood watching the dissolves, turning his gaze from screen to screen as each new pic came into focus. And he was starting to see something more there than just so many giga-pixels. She had an eye. Nothing posed or forced or overly cute. But there was affection in some shots, and distaste in others. The emotion bled through into the shot somehow.

"It's an emotional progression," he said, surprised at both the fact and at his ability to see it. The shots were arranged without seeming regard to subject category, but rather according to the mood expressed by the photographer's choices. The screens were moving from affection, to indifference, to active distaste or even contempt, to lust.

"What does that say?" he wondered aloud. "Contempt leads to lust? That can't be right."

But now the alternating shots were progressing to humor, to admiration, to a shot of him.

"Huh?" Jobs said, blinking fast and reaching un-consciously for some sort of freeze-frame. But then the shot of him was gone.

"That was off a pinhole camera," he muttered. The shot had come from a concealed camera, and he had a sinking feeling he knew when and where the shot had been taken. He'd had a look in his eyes: scared, hungry, hopeful, and scared some more.

He walked over to her computer and tapped at the keyboard. It asked for a code word. It took him twenty seconds to break the security and another twenty to run a word search for his own name. He popped a blank disc — he hoped it was blank, any-way — into the drive and copied the files.

This was highly immoral. But then, so was using a pinhole camera. Her wrong had necessitated his wrong. That wasn't a morally defensible position, but hey, this was love and wasn't all fair in love and war?

There was a noise from the hallway. Footsteps. Heavy ones. Jobs stifled a desperate yelp and dove for the window. He was halfway out, with his legs kicking to find a support when the light in the room snapped on.

"Who are you and what are you doing here?"

A man. Almost certainly Cordelia's father. With a stun gun. Not deadly but *very* painful.

"Um . . ."

"I would answer if I were you," the man said.

"My name is Jobs. I'm a friend of Cordelia's. From school. I was . . . See, she asked me to drop by and study with her."

A click. The man lowered his weapon. "I see. And she asked you to come in through the back window?"

Of course. In this position it looked like he'd been caught crawling in. That was something, at least. Cordelia's father didn't know he'd already been inside.

"I wasn't totally clear on where exactly she wanted me to come in."

"Uh-huh. Well, that makes perfect sense, son. Yes, I can see why you'd be confused: door, window, hard to keep them straight. Anyway, Cordy's not here. She's up in San Francisco for a couple days for her cousin's wedding."

"Ah."

"You can go now. And put the lawn furniture back where it belongs, hear me?"

Jobs climbed down. Mo'Steel was standing between two men in dark business suits.

"FBI," one of the men announced unnecessarily.

"Hi."

"We'll drive you boys home now."

"Okay."

The agent, a gray-haired man named Boxer, shook his head sadly. He patted Jobs's shoulder and said, "That's okay, son: You tried. Everyone wants to be a hero. It just ain't that kind of situation, that's all. It's just not hero time."

(CHAPTER SEVEN)

"NO ONE MAY SURVIVE."

2Face prepared to leave the house in the same way she had every morning for the last couple of months. She dressed, made sure everything necessary was in her pouch, checked the battery charge on her link. And then she stood in front of the mirror and looked at her face, looked at it long and hard.

No deception, that was the point. No fooling herself.

She turned to the right, showing her left face: the smooth, olive skin, the unsettling juxtaposition of pale gray eye color beneath distinctly Asian eyelid. The strong chin, the too-pert nose.

Then she turned the other way, revealing the burned, melted flesh. The eyelid drooped at the outside corner, making it seem the eye was eternally crying. Her cheek was like some aerial shot of a desert: pale ridges like sand dunes. Human caramel.

The nose was untouched, but beneath her long black hair the right ear was nearly gone, a nub. The hearing on that side was an echo chamber, hollow.

Her straight black hair was an illusion in part, grown longer on the top so she could conceal the ear and the fact that her hairline on that side began two inches higher than it once did.

But that was the only trick she allowed. She would not wear shades to hide the damaged eye. She would not wear a scarf to conceal the melted wax skin that extended down her neck as far as her collarbone.

This is what she looked like, at least till the next surgery. She had been beautiful all her life, naturally so, blessed by the fortuitous arrangement of the four letters along her DNA helix.

And then, the fire. And the hideous results. And the change in how people reacted to her.

It was fascinating. It was a lesson that no book taught. It was a spy-cam straight into the human soul. Everyone flinched when they saw her, that was to be expected, that was inevitable. How could they not? The human mind was prepared to see certain things and not others. So it wasn't the shocked looks that fascinated 2Face, rather it was what came next: the pity, the avoidance, the anger, the poor attempts to conceal disgust, the dishonesty, the bending over backward to pretend it wasn't there, and the outright ridicule and anger.

The anger was most interesting. People were outraged that she would dare to show them something ugly. It was a social sin. Her existence forced people to confront the uncertainty of life. And of course the irony disturbed people most of all: the pretty girl turned ugly. Like they would have understood if she'd been ugly to begin with. But a beauty turned hideous? What kind of rotten trick was that?

Her birth name was Essence Hwang. Before the fire she'd been called either SE for Essie, or Water-Baby, depending on whether it was a family member or someone from school. But once the bandages were unwrapped she knew she had to either hide from the truth or get right up in its face. She changed her name to 2Face. People thought it was rude, like she was forcing them to look.

Maybe so, maybe it was rude. But she had learned a lot, most of it not encouraging. She almost welcomed the whole thing, except for the hideous pain she'd endured earlier.

Almost.

She was stabilized, her health had been rebuilt, her scarred lungs were fully functional again. She was ready to start the series of reconstructive surgeries in exactly twenty-two days.

A year from now the doctors said she'd have her old face back, all of it, all of the eye-catching loveliness.

She'd wondered if she should refuse the surgery. That old face felt like a mask now. Maybe she should go through life as 2Face, proud, defiant, a living reproach to superficiality.

"No," she told the mirror sadly. "You're not that brave."

She headed downstairs intending to go running. She ran four miles a day. She hated it, but it was part of staying strong for the trauma of the operations. Part of strengthening her lungs. She would have preferred to swim, she'd been on the swim team back in the before, but chlorine burned her still-too-tender scar tissue in places.

She wore a running shark suit, skintight black from neck to ankles. She twisted her pouch around to the rear position, then pinned her link in place; the earpiece had a tendency to slip off. Heavy-use athletic links usually rested on two ears and she only had the one.

She paused at the top of the stairs and stretched, using the stairs themselves to lengthen leg muscles.

Then down the stairs at a quick trot, a nod to her dad in the kitchen, and past him toward the front door.

"Essie!" he called.

She paused, trotting in place to warm up and to demonstrate her impatience to be gone. "What?"

Her father walked over to her and clumsily put his arms around her, hugging her tight. Her dad was old-country Chinese, though he'd been a U.S. citizen for fifteen years; not a hugger, definitely not a hugger.

2Face pulled off her link and gently pushed her father back. "What's the matter, Daddy? Is it Mom? Is something the matter with Mom?"

"No, no, your mom is fine. She's on her way home. She ran out to get a few things. Listen, something is happening. Something very bad is happening."

He was agitated. Overwhelmed even. All 2Face could think was that it was her mother. What else would make her dad this upset?

The fire. He'd learned about the fire. He knew.

No, that was impossible. She couldn't start getting jumpy now.

"Daddy, tell me the truth: Has something happened to Mommy?"

He shook his head and drew her with him into the living room. It was the most formal room in the house: spare to the point of austerity. Three big flatscreens showed art that changed with the time of day. The furniture was low-slung, elongated, modern. Uncomfortable.

2Face sat perched beside her father, turned toward him. She consciously sat this way so her undamaged side was facing him. She didn't mind provoking strangers, but her pain had been felt too deeply by her father.

"I have the biggest story of my life," he said. "The biggest story of anyone's life."

"A story?" This was about some story? Her father was a producer for ABC news here in Miami. He worked closely with the network's investigative reporter, Carl Ramirez. "You're scaring me half to death over some work thing?"

She said it in a teasing tone, but her father's scared, serious expression didn't flicker.

Just then the door opened. 2Face's mother, Dawn Schulz-Hwang, came rushing in carrying two bags from the drugstore. Her mother said, "I got the toothbrushes. Q-Tips. Deodorant. Travel-pack sizes, except for your migraine pills, Shy."

She was agitated. 2Face's worry deepened. Why was her mother running out to buy travel-size toothpaste at this hour of the morning?

"It'll be okay, hon," Shy Hwang said. He turned back to his daughter. "We've had this story we were trying to get a grip on. We thought it was probably nothing. Rumor. Crazy stuff. But I told Carl I wanted to stay on it, I had a feeling about it. I didn't think it would be true, and it wasn't, not exactly. The story was that NASA had developed human hibernation technology and was going to use the technology to pull off a manned mission to Europa. You know, a moon of Jupiter."

"Yes, I know the moons of Jupiter," 2Face said impatiently.

"But that wasn't it. I reached this source, this guy who owed me a favor. He wouldn't talk except to give me a name: *Mayflower*. I used that name in a couple of places and all of a sudden word is coming down from on high to lay off. Then I reached out to the right person. She gave me chapter and verse. Chapter and verse and documentation."

"About a mission to Europa?" 2Face asked.

"No. That's a cover story. *Mayflower* is not about a mission to Europa. *Mayflower* is about a shuttle they're rigging up with hibernation berths for eighty people. Actually seventy-eight people plus two crew."

"Why on Earth would they be doing that?" his daughter asked.

"Because in three days an asteroid twice the size of Long Island is going to impact Earth," he said. "It will be the dinosaurs all over again. It's possible that the planet may literally break apart. No one may survive."

There was a long silence.

"Some other guys got parts of the story a couple days ago, ran with it, but they had no proof, so the story's dead. Me, I had the proof. But I spiked the story," Shy Hwang said.

"What? People have a right to know," 2Face said.

He shook his head. "No. If I had run with the story NASA would be mobbed with people trying to get on that shuttle. I killed the story in exchange for their agreement."

"What agreement?"

"I buried the story, and we go on that shuttle. Three berths. For the three of us."

"What? When? How soon?" 2Face asked, and unconsciously touched her marred cheek.

"Soon," her father said, unable to meet her gaze. "Too soon."

There was a knock at the front door and 2Face's mother spilled the drugstore bag.

CHAPTER EIGHT

"WHERE EXACTLY ARE WE GOING?"

They didn't kick the door down; they were more polite than that. But when Special Agent Boxer, with two other FBI agents and two DSA agents in tow arrived at the Andreeson home, they were the Mongol hordes showing up for breakfast unannounced.

"Ma'am, FBI," Boxer said, and promptly pushed past Jobs's mother, who was still chewing a toaster strudel and still in her bathrobe. The agents wore dark business suits, not the FBI logo windbreakers that Old Navy had begun to copy and sell for forty-two dollars.

The Data Security Agency agents wore office-casual clothes — that was their look.

The FBI agents, two men and one woman, went through the house, polite but relentless, gathering up papers, floppies, nubs, links, and the schoolbooks of Jobs and his brother. The DSA agents plopped themselves down in front of Jennifer Andreeson's computer and Jobs's computer. His mom's computer was networked with the house system's and all the other machines except for Jobs's own, which he had firewalled.

Edward was six, so he didn't burst out crying, but he did run to his mother and hug her knee, while she went hobbling after the agents saying, "Is this really necessary? Isn't this awfully early? I assumed you'd be here at a civilized hour. What are you doing? Put that down this instant."

Jobs was interested to observe that his mother's "or else!" voice did not work on FBI agents.

Tony Andreeson, Jobs's dad, was still asleep when an FBI woman hit the lights and announced herself.

"Uh-huh. Could you do it more quietly?" Jobs's dad grumbled. He was a software aestheticist and had the sort of job where no one expected you to show up early. Or at all.

"Sir, you need to get up and get dressed. You have thirty minutes. Pack a small bag, like carry-on luggage size. No electronics of any type. If you need more we can send for it later."

"Where exactly are we going?"

"That information is unavailable," the agent said with a bland smile.

Jobs had already stuffed a few T-shirts into a bag and now he stood watching as the DSA guy searched his computer files and his Web files.

"Pretty good encryption on some of these," the DSA agent said.

"Thanks. Not good enough, obviously."

The DSA man tapped away on the keyboard. He frowned. Looked back at Jobs, who kept his face carefully expressionless.

"Very cute: ghost files. I could hack in, but you could save me the time."

Ghost files were files hidden within regular files. They used the regular file as camouflage. Jobs leaned over and used the calculator for a moment, then typed in a number-letter code.

"Pi to six places divided by yesterday's date I get," the agent said. "What were the interposed letters?"

"A girl's name," Jobs said, hoping he sounded cool, not pathetic. "Cordelia."

"Uh. The girl from last night. She's a babe, huh?"

The ghost file opened. It contained the file he'd stolen from Cordelia's computer. It was video from a pinhole camera. She'd been wearing a pinhole cam on the night they'd kissed. That was where she'd gotten the scared close-up of him.

But it wasn't like that, he'd realized, after viewing the data the first time. Cordelia had been hired to do video of the dance for the school's zine. She'd been wearing a privacy warning button. It had come off during her angry encounter with her now ex-boyfriend. She probably didn't know that. Anyway, Jobs was prepared to believe she didn't know. Maybe didn't even know she was still shooting.

The DSA agent speed-scanned the video for a few seconds, got to the hideous moment when a sped-up Jobs leaned close for the great kiss that now seemed more comic than romantic, then closed the file without comment.

"She . . . Cordelia was . . ." Jobs started to explain.

The DSA agent shook his head. He was young for an agent, maybe fifteen years older than Jobs himself, though mostly bald. "Don't worry, kid, you got nothing here that's going to shock me. She pin-holed you, you swiped the file. Fair enough, right?"

No, that wasn't the way it was, Jobs wanted to say. But of course that's exactly how it was, at least on the surface. The kiss had meant everything to him when it lived only in memory. He should not have had to see it again. He should not have had to share it with a stranger. It should not be electronically stored data.

From the living room came his mother's cry, "What about the cats? I can't just leave them."

"They'll be taken care of, ma'am." A lie. Jobs knew it was a lie clear in the other room. Of course his mother did, too, but she broke down crying at that point, and Edward hugged her.

Tony Andreeson said, "For God's sake, Jen, you don't even like the cats."

"Let me put food out for them. Let me at least do that. Oh, Digit's already so fat, if I leave out all this food . . . the vet will . . ."

Jobs met the DSA agent's gaze. "You know what all this is about, sir?" Jobs asked.

The agent said, "Officially, no."

Jobs nodded. He tried to think of something pithy to say, maybe something about the irony of his mother crying over a pair of cats when the whole world was coming to an end. But all he managed was, "It's kind of disturbing."

"Yeah," the DSA guy said. And then he unhooked his link from his belt, tapped the screen, and showed Jobs a picture of three kids, all young, ranging maybe from two to six. The agent seemed about to say something, then lost focus as he gazed at the softly glowing photo.

Jobs considered whether he should reveal the encrypted files he'd programmed to transfer into the DSA agent's decryption program. They were harmless files, not viruses, created only to prove he could do it, not to cause damage.

No. It would hurt the guy's feelings. No adult liked being outwitted by a teenager. And the guy had enough on his mind. He would be dead soon. Him, his wife, his three kids, everyone he cared about.

"I better go see if I can help my mom and dad," Jobs said. There was nothing he could say to this man. Nothing the maybe survivor could possibly say to the surely dead.

"Yeah." Then the agent shook himself free of the picture and said, "Hey, you have some writing in here, looks like poems. You want a printout to take with you?"

Jobs shook his head. "No. None of it's any good. Besides . . ." He let the thought hang, unable to find any way to explain the deep sense that the one way, the only way to do this was with a clean break. A bright clear line between a past already suffused with nostalgic golden light, and a terrible, desperate future. "No. Thanks."

Forty-five minutes after the FBI agents arrived, the Andreeson family was bundled into a dark-colored Suburban with black-out windows accompanied by a dark sedan and a windowless white van.

They drove down familiar streets. Jobs looked out the window and knew beyond any doubting that he would never see this home, this street, this place again.

Two blocks away they passed Mo'Steel's house. A black Suburban, a black sedan, and a white van were parked in the front. Inside Mo'Steel's house, in his room, some DSA agent would be going through his computer, unable to believe the nearly untouched, pristine emptiness of the thing.

"What do you mean you don't have any personal files? None? Have you ever even turned this thing on?"

That thought brought a smile to Jobs's face.

Edward was playing with a pair of action figures, making soft *boosh, boosh* explosion sounds.

Where would the Rock hit? Would it hit far out in the ocean and send a wave to wash this idyllic place into the sea like a sand castle with the tide coming in?

Would the Rock hit far across the planet and break the world apart, sending unimaginably huge wedges spinning off into space? Would this place, his place, still be intact when the sea boiled away, when the atmosphere ghosted away leaving the few still-living creatures to gasp in vacuum?

Maybe the Rock would hit right here, *boom,* right on top of them. Maybe it would come ripping through the puffy clouds, scattering the fog, a hurricane wind rushing before it. Slam right here into this very place.

He thought of asking his mother. She was in the seat in front of him. She would know, if anyone would. But she was crying softly. Jobs reached to put his hand on her shoulder. And once again, words failed him.

He thought too much about what he ought to say, he knew that. He looked too long for the perfect words and ended up saying nothing at all. But what did you say at the end of the world?

(CHAPTER NINE)

"YOU HAVE TO ASSUME THOSE TWO KIDS ARE ARMED AND DANGEROUS."

A private jet took the Andreeson and Gonzalez families, Jobs and Mo'Steel, their respective parents, plus Edward, from the tiny Monterey Airport to a refueling stop in the middle of nowhere west Texas, then on to Cape Canaveral, Florida.

A limousine hauled 2Face and her family from Miami, up the coast past blazing white beaches and sun-roasted tourists.

In San Jose and Austin and Houston and Seattle, in Boston and Washington and New York, the FBI and DSA descended suddenly and swept up their charges and hustled them aboard the unmarked jets borrowed from the Defense Department.

D-Caf and his brother, Mark, had to provide their own transportation, a regular commercial flight out of Baltimore-Washington International airport that landed in Miami. Then they caught a bus northward.

They used false identification that Mark had created. They used a credit card number plucked off the Web. It would be hours before the FBI realized that one of the many "Aware Individuals" had disappeared.

Special Agent Paul Boxer had followed Jobs's family to their destination, then been detached to Miami along with half the field agents in the United States. The Miami office would oversee coverage for the Kennedy Space Center. Boxer drew the assignment to locate and question Mark Melman and his brother, D-Caf. Mark Melman was known to be cognizant of the Mayflower Project.

Boxer requested that the Baltimore office search the Melman home. They found evidence of the flight to Miami. And worse.

Boxer took the call while eating his third hot, fresh, practically melting Krispy Kreme doughnut.

"They're in the Miami area, that's definite," the Baltimore agent reported. "They're all yours, Paul."

"Great. What do we know about this guy? Anything that's not in the file?"

"We canvassed the neighbors. They all say the same: Mark is a nice guy, but a loner. His little brother, who calls himself D-Caf, is kind of a twitchy kid. One other big thing, though: Their father had a weapon."

"A weapon?"

"A Ruger six-shot .44 magnum. And it's missing. You have to assume those two kids are armed and dangerous."

The news did not particularly surprise or bother Agent Boxer. The lunatic fringe had never bought the official denials of the Mayflower Project. The nuts were gathering around Cape Canaveral. Where there were nuts, there were guns; the two went hand-in-hand.

And really, with all the so-called militias, all the doomsday cults, the extremists, and the outright terrorists, some maladjusted computer geek and his twitchy brother didn't seem like a top-level threat.

Boxer had another doughnut. He'd fought a weight problem all his life. Well, if there was one up-side to the end of the world it was that now, at least, he could eat all the Krispy Kremes he wanted.

CHAPTER TEN

"TICKTOCK, HERE COMES THE ROCK."

The chosen few, the eighty men, women, and children who would form the cargo of the *Mayflower*, were taken to a remote corner of the base, to a shabby, run-down, long-abandoned barracks. It was one of three barracks buildings which, together with a low administrative bungalow, an olive-drab mess tent, and a perilously leaning motor-pool barn formed a sort of compound.

The only thing new in the compound was the chain-link fence topped with razor wire.

One of the Eighty had arrived a few hours early. His birth name was Robert Castleman. He called himself Yago.

The President of the United States, Janice Castleman, had refused a berth for herself and her husband. But she had demanded, and been given, a berth for their fifteen-year-old son.

And as Yago stood contemplating the noisy squalor of the barracks, the disorder of arriving families, he knew beyond any reasonable doubt that his parents had secured his berth not so much to save his life as to have him out of theirs.

That would hurt, Yago thought, *if I cared.*

Yago had never been a good politician's child. Articles had been written about him, contrasting him unfavorably with the sainted Chelsea Clinton, dean of Perfect Presidential Children (who had, of course, gone on to be such a spectacularly, tediously perfect adult), but also mentioning Amy Carter and John-John Kennedy and various others going all the way back to Lincoln's kids. No one could come up with another presidential kid quite like Yago.

Polls showed that Yago had actually earned his mother a fair number of sympathy votes following the fateful interview in which, at age thirteen, he'd told the NBC news anchor his goal in life was to become "feared."

Then there had been the time he yelled, "Gun!" at the top of his lungs during a post-summit meeting press conference. The Secret Service had tackled his mother, and the security detail around the president of Azerbaijan had very nearly shot a sound man holding a long microphone that looked just a bit like a rifle.

Yago surveyed a glum assemblage, for the most part, these chosen survivors. They had all packed in a hurry, hustled along by FBI agents. There were too few toothbrushes and not enough toilet paper and everyone was hungry and all the littler kids wanted upper bunks, and all the parents wanted lower bunks, and where was the trash, and good lord why wasn't it air-conditioned, and why couldn't they at least have killed the roaches, and how were they supposed to have any privacy at all?

"Killing time till it's killing time," Yago muttered and laughed a bit at his bon mot. Normally he'd have recorded it on his link. But it was an unhooked, un-linked world now. It made him feel deaf and blind. A creepy feeling.

There were no really young kids. There was no set cutoff age. But, prepubescent kids were thought to be at greater risk from hibernation. There were no old people, either. The upper age limit was just over forty. It wasn't just that NASA wanted everyone to be fit and healthy, they were also looking ahead: to populating some entirely speculative planet.

But in a room filled with scientists and the kids of scientists you couldn't ignore facts: The *Mayflower* didn't represent a real chance, it represented death delayed. Or death unnoticed, unremarked: Death deprived of all the drama and majesty of the shatter-ing, fiery annihilation that was being prepared by that cold-blooded killer Mother Nature.

For his part Yago had no doubts. He had a des-tiny. His destiny was not to die on a shattered Earth, one of seven-billion bugs cowering under the big cosmic shoe. Nor was it to float through the cold emptiness of space for the remaining life of the uni-verse, pockmarked by micrometeorites and disinte-grated into soup by radiation.

Yago was going to be something. And there was no point moping over the long odds, or boo-hooing over poor, lost Earth. The point was to figure out how to come out on top. And the time to start preparing was now.

He fixed his gaze on the most promising arrival, the Asian girl, the one with the messed-up face. She would be an easy mark. Like taking candy from a baby.

He tried to recall her name from the personnel files he'd wheedled out of a secretary at the White House. What was it . . . Scent? No, that couldn't be it. Substance . . . Effect . . . Essence! That was it: Essence Hwang.

Well, it was her lucky day.

Yago knew he was good-looking. After all, he got

fan mail from half the girls in the United States, and a lot of girls from other countries, too. They even sent pictures, and some of them weren't half bad.

He was tall and powerfully built. He had his dad's Caucasian, male-model features and his mother's African-American skin coloration, but the rest of his "look" was straight out of a petri dish — his parents were rich and indulgent.

Yago had had his original kinky hair replaced with straight-growing light brown hair, which he'd dyed different colors over time — it was currently the green of a late-summer elm leaf. His original brown eyes had been genetically altered to a distinctly golden color with just enough cat DNA to be slightly reflective in the dark. His teeth were unnaturally white and perfectly straight. His skin would never know a pimple. He'd even had his navel relocated and reshaped.

The smirk was all his own.

He was handsome, he was smart, he was smooth: He was way, way out of the freak-girl's league, obviously. But if he beamed the sunlight of his attention on her she'd be his devoted servant not only now, but later, when they all thawed out. And that was the key: He would need a hard core of sycophants ready to back him up from the very first.

He'd seen the early documents on the Mayflower Project. He'd seen right away what everyone
else in their desperate haste had missed: There was
no one in charge. No hierarchy. No one in command.

How could they be dumb enough not to see that
wherever the *Mayflower* ended up, someone would
be giving orders? What did the NASA people think?
That they'd form up into Democrats and Republi-
cans and hold an election?

In any crisis the strong rose to the top and the
weak fulfilled their own paltry destiny as willing ser-
vants, unwilling slaves, or victims.

It was a game. A hard, cruel game of survival, and
he at least understood that. Let the others mope
for poor old Earth. He was starting the game early:
right now.

"Kind of a zoo, huh?" Yago said.

Essence Hwang looked at him thoughtfully. Like
he looked familiar, but she couldn't quite place him.
"I guess it is," she said. Adding, "Literally."

"I'm Yago," he said and flashed his number-two
modest smile — not the full, number-three aw-
shucks modesty he saved for meeting with sports
stars, but more than the deliberately transparent
number-one modesty. He made a sort of deprecat-

ing gesture toward the two Secret Service agents, Horvath and Jackson, who watched him from a discreet distance. "Don't mind those guys. They come with the job." He raised his voice. "As a matter of fact, why don't you guys take five, huh? I don't think I'm in any danger."

The girl glanced at the departing agents, obviously clicked into recognition, and said, "Oh. I'm 2Face." She watched him closely, waiting to gauge his reaction.

He gave her nothing. He'd long ago learned to conceal all but the strongest emotions. "So, what do you think of all this? Kind of amazing, isn't it?"

2Face considered. "It seems very sad to me."

The girl looked like she might start crying. Or maybe that was just the creepy way her messed-up eye always looked. He wished she'd turn her head a little, not aim all that scar tissue at him.

Yago nodded. "It's very sad. The whole Earth getting wiped out and all. Ticktock, here comes the Rock. All those people dying and whatnot. Kind of depressing. So, you here with your folks?"

"Yes. My mom and dad."

"Me, I'm alone," Yago said. "You know, my mom's the president, so she has this idea she has to go down with the ship. Like that's going to help all the losers who're getting sledgehammered into the center of Earth. I think she can't get it out of her head that she's not exactly running for reelection."

Yago laughed a winning laugh, expecting 2Face to join in. She didn't. In fact she gave every sign of wishing she was somewhere else.

"I hope we can be friends," Yago said. He'd spent his life around politicians, and could, when it was required, mimic the heartfelt tone, the sincere look, even the warm handshake. He could also mimic the subtle threat. "Wherever we end up, a girl like you will need friends."

"I see. A girl like me. Do you want to be my boyfriend?"

Yago gulped, caught off-guard for once. "Do I . . ." He almost laughed. The idea that the freak was going to be his girlfriend was just amazing. Who did she think she was?

2Face winked with her one good eye and smiled a smile that was unavoidably wry. "Sell it somewhere else," she said, and started to walk away.

Yago grabbed her shoulder, spun her back to face him. "Hey, freak. You don't turn your back on me till I say you can go."

2Face tried to knock his hand away but Yago had a powerful grip. She struck at him, palm outward, trying to push him away.

It was a blow, clearly, clearly, in Yago's mind, it was a blow. She had hit him! All bets were off, all restraint was gone. She'd hit him!

Yago drew back his hand to deliver a slap. Two hands locked around his wrist. Yago glared, processed the necessary data: It was the nerd. The one from California. What was the name? Oh, yeah.

"No," Jobs said. He shook his head slightly. "No."

Yago glared at this intruder. He wasn't very big and he didn't look very tough. He looked scared. But he didn't flinch or look away.

Yago rotated his hand, broke Jobs's grip, and using the same hand, shot a short, hard, snapping punch into Jobs's head.

Jobs fell back. Yago shoved hard and knocked him on his butt.

2Face yelled, "Stop it! Stop it, you jerk!"

Yago moved in to kick Jobs. He would teach the punk a valuable lesson. Once they're down, make sure they stay down.

Just then, a blur of movement: someone running, bounding from top bunk to top bunk.

"Yaaahhh!"

Mo'Steel threw himself at Yago, caught him around the neck, and carried him to the floor.

Yago rolled with almost professional skill and was on his feet in a flash. But so were Jobs and Mo'Steel and 2Face. Three against one.

Yago spotted the Secret Service agents across the room drinking coffee from disposable cups. "They attacked me!" he roared. "What are you do-ing standing there? They attacked me! Get them. Get them!"

The agent named Horvath looked puzzled. He cupped a hand to his ear and pantomimed that he couldn't hear. Agent Jackson just smiled.

Yago swallowed the rage that came boiling up inside him. Swallowed it hard and slowly, slowly erased the feral, murderous expression from his face.

"We seem to have a misunderstanding," he said stiffly, then turned and walked away. Under his breath he added, "On my list. That's three of you, on my list."

(CHAPTER ELEVEN)

"SHE LAKKA YOU BEEZNESS."

"You want me to go bounce on him some more?" Mo'Steel asked Jobs.

"No. Let it go. It's all over." Jobs put a hand on Mo'Steel's arm and gently drew him away.

2Face said, "Hey. Thanks."

Jobs shrugged. "No problem."

"No, I mean, really: Thanks. Is your head okay?"

Jobs touched his injured ear and then looked at his hand. There was a little blood on his fingers. It seemed to puzzle him. "Hmm."

"You should have someone look at that. You need a Band-Aid," 2Face said.

"That ear is gonna have to come off," Mo'Steel offered with a giddy grin. "Get you a nice, new, titanium ear. Change your name to . . . to, um, oh, hey, I know! Change your name to Earanium!"

Jobs and 2Face both looked at him. "Earanium?"

"Hey, it's the best I could come up with just off the top of my head, all right? You know, you're not exactly Mr. Quick either," Mo'Steel grumbled.

"This is my friend Mo," Jobs said. "Mo'Steel. I'm Jobs. And the ear is fine. Mo's in favor of as much surgery as possible."

"2Face."

They shook hands. The name brought a smile to Jobs's face. He nodded to himself, absorbing it, smiled again.

Jobs looked at her face, interested at almost a scientific level in the effect. Not at all horrified, not at all sickened.

"I was in a fire," she said.

He nodded. "Yeah. Well, see you later."

For his part Jobs had already half forgotten the incident. He was remembering the girl instead. His always-distracted expression grew positively dreamy.

"That girl liked your business, Duck."

"What?"

"Uh-uh, don't give me 'what?'" Mo'Steel said. "You know what I said. She lakka you beeznees. She wants to invest in you."

Jobs said, "Mo, you know I'm faithful to Cordelia."

"The girl who isn't even totally sure who you are?"

Jobs smiled ruefully. Cordelia knew who he was, he was sure of that at least. She'd included his picture in her flatscreen montage. He'd come in right after what, admiration? But what had come next? He couldn't remember, had been too stunned to pay attention. Where did he fit in Cordelia's emotional cycle?

No way he could go into that with Mo. Mo was an old-fashioned kid. He'd never understand creeping Cordelia's computer. Jobs said, "Yeah. That's right, Mo: Cordelia, the girl who isn't sure who I am."

"That's you, Jobs: All you need is a girlfriend up here." He tapped his head. "Me, I need a real, live girl. You know, like maybe someone who would recognize me at least."

"What's going to happen to her?" Jobs asked, but silently, to himself alone. "What will happen to Cordelia?"

Had to avoid those images. Had to sheer off, stay out of that, or lose his mind. The Rock was coming. Cordelia was just another dinosaur.

He shook his head so hard that Mo'Steel looked at him with concern.

"What's the bruise, compadre?"

"They didn't leave us any hope, Mo. The Rock. It's all too sure. Too . . . And we don't get to fight it, man. All we can do is run away. All we can do is be cowards and save ourselves. It's just random. If the Rock's trajectory was one-hundredth of a degree different, it'd miss us. It's just random, and we don't even get to fight it. What kind of a story is that?"

Mo'Steel looked perplexed. Then he shrugged. "Maybe we fight later, Duck."

"It can't all end this way. It can't just end in some meaningless . . ." Jobs couldn't find the word. He hung his head. "Everyone's just going to die, Mo. What's the point in that?"

Mo'Steel said, "Everyone always dies, man. Always been that way. And I don't think it ever did have a point. Did it?"

CHAPTER TWELVE

"OH, MY GOD, ALL THOSE PEOPLE."

Cordelia was in San Francisco. Actually standing on the balcony of a monstrously big faux-Victorian mansion atop exclusive Twin Peaks. The balcony looked out over the backyard where the wedding reception of her cousin, Lucy, was under way. But more compelling by far, to her artist's eye, was the view beyond the backyard.

The house had been built on two lots. Two existing houses had been torn down to make room, and to ensure the capture of this very view.

The view included much of San Francisco, down through the skyscrapered downtown and beyond to the sparkling bay, ornamented by the eternally stunning Golden Gate Bridge. As it happened, an aircraft carrier, the new, sleek, low-silhouette USS *Reagan*, was entering the bay, sliding beneath the bridge in a spectacle that combined the reassuring grace of perfect form with the disturbing grace of might.

Of course Cordelia was supposed to be focusing her link on the reception. She had the latest link, capable of shooting very high-resolution video and transmitting it directly to satellite, so she'd been drafted, or perhaps volunteered, she wasn't sure which, to act as the videographer. The link allowed far-flung family members to follow the events live from anywhere they happened to be.

Messages were beginning to pile up, superimposed on the viewfinder. Messages like, "Show the ceremony!" And, "We want to see the bride, not the bridge!!!" Cordelia ignored them. The more they nagged, the less she was going to show the silly bride and her dweeb of a groom.

Cordelia's cousin was from a very wealthy family, money derived from the biotech boom. Cordelia herself came from a more modest background. A more restrained background. Not cheap, not puritanical, just reasonable. Her family did not believe in ostentatious displays of wealth. Her family would not have placed twelve-thousand dollars' worth of Beluga caviar in seventeen-thousand dollars' worth of crystal and then gone about ten steps too far by covering each mound of caviar with edible gold foil.

Okay, so Lucy's family had money. Did they have to rub people's noses in it?

And yet, for this view ... What wouldn't Cordelia do to be able to look out at this magnificence every day?

Maybe she'd be rich someday. Maybe she'd be a really rich photographer. Uh-huh. There were about, hmm, two rich photographers.

Maybe she'd marry a rich guy. Jobs would probably make a lot of money some day; he was shockingly smart after all. Of course that was jumping the gun a little bit, but that's what weddings did to you: made you go all mushy and misty and begin fantasizing.

Her dad had called to tell her that he'd caught Jobs trying to crawl in her bedroom window. That was either very romantic or insane or some combination of the two. Romeo or Psycho? He could be nuts, that was a possibility to consider.

Jobs was definitely different. He'd spent close to half an hour listening to her, actually listening, without trying to make the conversation about himself. And he'd made no move on her. Just listened. The number of guys Cordelia had met in her entire life who could actually listen intelligently was, well, one.

Unfortunately, setting aside the odd home-invasion, Jobs seemed to have no follow-up. He hadn't asked her out, despite the fact he was definitely interested. So, she'd have to ask him out. Only, check with people at school first and find out if he was actively crazy.

Her link was ringing. Again.

"Yes?" Cordelia asked in an innocent singsong.

It was her great-aunt Rebecca (formerly great-uncle Robert). "Cordelia, honey, show us the bride and groom or —"

"— Sorry, your audio is breaking up." She killed the connection. Then she turned the link around to show herself standing before the view and laughing.

She was not a classically beautiful girl; her face had too much character for that. Her nose was too big, for one thing. She'd thought of having it fixed, but hey, it was a family trait. Her hair was blond — actual blond, not petri-dish blond, and she wore it long. Her eyes were authentically blue.

She winked at the link, knowing she was really annoying her extended family now.

"Okay, okay, I'll show the bride," she said.

She started to pan down toward the reception again, intending to focus on the rather gruesome sight of Lucy stuffing her face with crab legs, but something drew her eye.

In the sky.

It was a small asteroid, a meteorite, no more than eight-hundred feet in diameter, a chip that long ago had spun off the Rock in its collision with the comet.

Just a chip. A pebble.

It ripped through the air, shrieking, a hurricane wind behind it.

The pebble slammed into San Francisco Bay just short of hitting Alameda.

The explosion was equal to a nuclear weapon.

The entire contents of San Francisco Bay, billions upon billions of gallons of water shot skyward, a vast column of superheated steam. Millions of tons of dirt, the floor of the bay, erupted, a volcano.

The immediate shock wave flattened every building in Alameda and Oakland. Skyscrapers were simply knocked over like a kid's pile of blocks. Frame houses collapsed. Cars were tossed around like leaves in the wind.

The water of the bay surged in, sucking the USS *Reagan* into the bay, a swirling bath toy, then all at once the water blew back. The USS *Reagan* was picked up and thrown into and through the Golden Gate Bridge. The rust-red bridge wrapped bodily around the flying ship. The bridge supports ripped from the shores. Cable snapped like bullwhips.

The shock wave reached San Francisco itself. The downtown area pancaked. Areas that were landfill simply melted away, quick sand, entire square miles of the city sank down into the water.

A million dead in less than five seconds.

Cordelia said, "Oh, my God, all those people." It was all she had time to say before the shock wave ripped apart the mansion on Twin Peaks.

The final image broadcast was from a link lying sideways. The lens was speckled with dust. But the image was still clear: Cordelia lay on her side, her face shocked. She looked down and saw the two-by-four that had been driven through her chest. She shuddered and died.

(CHAPTER THIRTEEN)

"MAYBE THE WORLD IS COMING TO AN END,
IT DOESN'T MATTER: YOU FOLLOW ORDERS."

Sergeant Tamara Hoyle had a simple enough task: Protect the perimeter. A standard task for any Marine. Protect the perimeter of the compound from any unauthorized persons attempting to enter or depart.

She followed orders, deployed her Marines as she had been instructed to do by her captain, kept them alert, did her best to keep them focused on the job at hand. One or two of her Marines raised complaints, fears, wanted to know what kind of a mission this was, anyway, standing guard at the end of the world when they should be home with their families, after all what did any of it matter?

Sergeant Hoyle had taken time to explain patiently. "Excuse me, son? Did I hear you right?" she demanded, levering her body forward, bringing her angry, incredulous face to within a millimeter of the unfortunate private's nose. "You want to go home, Marine? Well, I guess you're just about the first Marine in all of history who has thought about that. All those guys who went ashore on Iwo Jima, Inchon, any of a hundred different places, getting chewed up on godforsaken beaches, I don't guess any of them ever thought maybe they'd rather be home drinking a cold beer."

"All due respect, Sarge, this is different."

"No, private, it isn't different. You're a Marine. You have your orders. You follow orders. Maybe you live, maybe you die, maybe you like it, maybe you don't, maybe the world is coming to an end, it doesn't matter: You follow orders. Is that clear?"

It was clear.

It was clear to the private. It was not clear to the sergeant.

Tamara Hoyle was twenty-two years old with two and a half years in the Corps. She was seven weeks pregnant, a fact she had not yet revealed to her husband, a Marine who was on embassy duty in Tokyo, or to her superiors. The Corps provided for an eighteen-month leave of absence in the event of pregnancy — time that had to be made up.

There would be no hiding it, of course. Tamara

Hoyle was five foot nine, one hundred and twenty pounds, with the kind of stomach you get from doing a hundred crunches every morning followed by fifty military push-ups and a five-mile run. You couldn't hide a pregnant belly on that kind of body.

Tamara Hoyle loved the Corps. She loved being a Marine. She believed everything she had ever heard (or said) about duty, honor, and country. And the Marine sergeant was determined that the end of the world would still find her little part of the Corps executing their lawful orders. *Semper Fi:* always faithful. Always.

Following orders had presented no conflicts between Tamara Hoyle the Marine and Tamara Hoyle the someday mother. The Marines guarding the compound had been fully briefed — it was thought they'd learn the truth anyway — and Sergeant Hoyle had accepted the fact that her baby would never be born. That there would, in all probability, be no world for her to be born into. That was like a bayonet to the heart, but there was no changing things, and orders were orders.

But then, that first evening as she stood at rest smoking a safe-cig in the dark outside the barracks, listening to the frogs and the crickets, a young woman emerged to stand beside her.

"You're pregnant," the young woman said.

Tamara nearly swallowed her safe-cig. The woman's voice carried such conviction that there was no denying. "How do you know?"

The woman stuck out a hand and Tamara shook it. "I'm Connie Huerta. Doctor Connie Huerta, OB-GYN. I'm wrong sometimes, but not often." She withdrew her hand and for the first time Tamara noticed the tiny medi-scan, no more than a thin film of plastic.

Doctor Huerta looked at the medi-scan, peered close to make out the tiny digital readout. "I'd say you're between six and eight weeks along."

Tamara took a deep, shaky breath, let it out slowly, recovered some of her inner calm. But the woman's next words blew away her calm entirely.

"Sergeant, I don't want to be here. I'm here with my husband. I don't love my husband. I love a guy . . . a guy. Leave it at that. I don't want to go on this trip. Me, I'd rather stay behind. Anyway, I'm a doctor: Maybe not everyone will be killed right away when the Rock hits. If there are people hurt I should be there."

"You're an obstetrician, not exactly a trauma surgeon," Tamara pointed out.

Connie smiled. "Yes. But if you're hurt I'll be better than no doctor at all. Besides, women will still be having babies. For a while. Maybe."

Tamara shook her head. "I have my orders. No one leaves the compound. Sorry." She used her no-nonsense voice, putting an end to the conversation.

But the doctor wasn't so easily cowed. She moved closer, to whispering distance. "We're much the same size, Sergeant. When they give us the word, you let me walk away, and you take my place. Use my berth." She placed her hand gently on Tamara's very slightly swollen belly. "You may save your baby."

Tamara removed the woman's hand, gently but firmly. "I'm a Marine, Doctor: I have my orders."

Connie Huerta started to say something more, but then she shrugged and let it go.

Tamara was relieved. It had been an unsettling encounter, but it was over.

Then she heard the cries.

She dropped her safe-cig and ran inside the barracks. Everyone was gathered around the TV in the common room.

"What is it?" she demanded. She had to repeat the question several times before getting an answer.

"San Francisco was just wiped out," a man said. "Some girl was filming it live. So much for the big secret."

CHAPTER FOURTEEN

"I'M NOT KILLING ANYONE,
THE ROCK IS KILLING THEM."

FBI agents led by Agent Boxer kicked in the door of the motel in Titusville, Florida. They found several pizza boxes, a number of empty cookie and candy bar wrappers, and the personal hygiene items belonging to Mark and Harlin Melman.

The TV was tuned to CNN, still doing San Francisco without letup. Showing the same satellite photos of a devastated Bay Area. Showing interviews with survivors from the fringe of the blast. Showing that awful link-video from a girl whose name was now known to every person left on Earth: Cordelia.

But neither Mark nor D-Caf were in the room, and no, the motel's phones had not been used to call for a taxi, and no, neither Mark nor D-Caf had accessed the Web or used their links in any way. A search of the trash found no telltale receipts. The stolen credit card number had not been used again.

So clearly the young man and the boy had "gone to cash," slipped off the Web, out of sight.

Just as clearly they were up to no good. There was no innocent explanation for the sudden disappearance of the prodigy Mark Melman and his little brother.

But they were not the only potential trouble-makers, or anything like the most serious, either. The FBI was strained to its limits. Agents had been brought in from all over the United States and even from stations abroad to keep an eye on the hundreds, if not thousands of people who knew about the Mayflower Project but had not been bought off with a boarding pass.

Mark's plan relied on his own deep knowledge of the Kennedy Space Center and the surrounding area. Part of his job had been to streamline the data flow from security sensors around the facility. The scruffy woods, with its stunted pines and dense thickets and humid bogs, was protected by a string of sensors: infrared, motion sensors, even microphones tuned to pick up human speech.

But these sensors were not — could not be — watched by human monitors. Instead the barrage of data was overseen by computers programmed to differentiate between a wild pig or a heron and a human.

Mark had left all the sensors functioning fully. The program itself would pass even the most rigorous tests. But Mark had played a little game with the program: He had created a sort of cloak of invisibility.

As he and D-Caf walked through the wild brush they had to contend with mosquitoes, with the possibility of snakes, and most of all with the innumerable falls and scrapes that resulted from walking in darkness when you're not used to night vision goggles.

D-Caf caught his right foot on a root and pitched forward into a bush. "Ow. Oh, snake! Snake!"

Mark grabbed him by the jacket collar and yanked him to his feet. "It's not a snake. Look: There's nothing there."

D-Caf stared at the spot where he'd fallen. It was green-on-green, but not the natural green of chlorophyll but the eerie, glowing green of the night-vision equipment. There was no snake, green or otherwise.

"There was one, he just ran off. Slithered off, I mean."

Mark nodded. "See, up in that tree? You can just make out the antenna. It's a sensor."

"Do you think they heard us?"

"Yes. Of course the sensor picked up your whining, and it sees our infrared and has registered your extremely clumsy movement. It would easily determine that we are humans except for the fact that we're putting off a very precisely tuned audio signal — too high for us to hear — but audible to the sensor." He tapped the signal generator clipped to his belt. "The computer is programmed to see anything putting off that audio signal as a wild pig, regardless of the other data."

"What would they do if they caught us?"

"Shoot us," Mark said harshly. Then, realizing that this would just set D-Caf off, he said, "Just kidding, Hamster. They'd just arrest us and kick us off the base."

D-Caf fell into step behind his brother, determined this time not to trip again, or to ask any more dumb questions. But it was creepy out here in the snake-infested woods, where every gnarled, dwarfish tree looked like some glowing, green, radioactive monster.

D-Caf slipped his goggles down to his chin. The moon was at the quarter and it gave barely adequate light. When the clouds scudded across it the light was almost entirely extinguished.

It wasn't quiet out here; there were endless insect and animal sounds, buzzing, rasping, croaking, and a weird, harsh cough that may have been anything.

"How much farther?" D-Caf asked.

"Half a mile."

"I need to rest."

"No. Do you just not get it? The ship launches tomorrow night: 2:26 in the morning. After that thing in San Francisco, that tape being on all the news shows, all over the world, this secret is not going to keep. They can talk accidental nuclear explosion and all that, but no one buys that load of bull: the only nukes were aboard the carrier, and it would have been vaporized, not flying backward through the bridge. People are figuring it out, which means everything is gonna hit the fan and security is going to come down even harder. There's no backup launch window, NASA has to go. This is it. Either we're on board, or we're dead."

D-Caf shrugged. "Maybe we shouldn't do it."

Mark spun and yanked his collar, yanked him close. "Don't even start."

"You said yourself it was a sham, Mark. I mean, if

it's not even going to save our lives then why do it? I mean, why? I can't kill someone."

"You won't have to," his brother sneered, releasing his angry hold. "I've always taken care of you, haven't I?"

"Yeah. You have. Ever since Mom and Dad. But you don't want to kill anyone, either, Mark. I know you don't."

"I'm not killing anyone, the Rock is killing them. If the Rock is going to kill everyone, how can I be a murderer, huh? Have you figured that out?"

Mark wasn't sure whether he wanted to roll up in a ball and be sick, or beat his brother's face in. The stupid kid! Didn't he realize how hard this was? Didn't he realize he was just making things worse? Mark was saving his stupid life, maybe, saving him from the end of the whole lousy world and all he could do was whine?

"We'll get caught," D-Caf wailed.

"Yeah? What are they going to do? Put us in jail for life? That's a twenty-seven-hour sentence."

"Doesn't make it right," D-Caf whispered.

"Hey, you saw the video. You saw what happened to the whole Bay Area? Everyone within five miles of the impact point is dead. That was a pebble, some little nothing knocked loose from the Rock. What happened there was a joke compared to what's happening in twenty-seven hours."

"We'll never make it," D-Caf said, sounding defeated. "It's the end. It's all going to end."

"Yeah? Then I guess you might as well relax. Let's go."

(CHAPTER FIFTEEN)

"YOU'LL BE THERE. YOU'LL BE THERE."

Jobs heard whimpering in the night. He was not asleep. Sleep wasn't possible. Cordelia. The link had shown her smiling, mugging for the camera, just moments before her link recorded the single most devastating natural disaster in human history.

He told himself she was alive. They couldn't know, not for sure. Everyone dead? Maybe that was just because they didn't want to try and save anyone.

Not that it mattered. She was dead now, or would die later. Dead from the Pebble, dead from the Rock. What was the difference? What did it matter?

The whimpering again, more urgent.

Was it Edward? The tape had shaken him, too. It had shaken everyone. It had made it all very, very real.

Jobs rolled sideways and looked across at Edward's bunk. It was just two feet away. Not Edward. His brother was snoring softly, clutching his pillow tight.

Jobs looked over the edge of the bunk, down at his dad. He felt weird doing so, like he was invading his parents' privacy. There was no privacy here, but still, he didn't have the right to look at his dad sleeping, at his mom in her own lower bunk. It was like sneaking into their room.

Like sneaking into someone's room and creeping their computer. God, why did his memory of Cordelia have to be tainted with all that? If he'd never had more than that one perfect kiss, if he and Cordelia had never been anything more to each other, he could have lived with that. Now his memories were fouled with feelings of guilt, with a sense of irrational resentment, all layered over, overwhelmed by those hideous images of death.

If she was still alive, if his own life was still to be lived, if, if, if, he could have discovered, they could have discovered . . . Maybe there would have been love. Maybe that. Maybe she would have loved him. Maybe what was wispy and slight could have become deep and enduring, real.

The whimpering came again, and for a moment

Jobs wondered if the sounds came from him. But the words were not in English. More guttural. Like a very young child's inflection. Like a kid trying to sound like a baby or something.

The room was dark but for the glowing red exit sign at either end of the room, the sliver of light from the bathroom, and the blue glow of the TV set at the far end of the room. A half dozen people sat hunched there, watching, watching, watching the only show on any channel: San Francisco.

Cordelia.

It was dark in the rest of the barracks, but not quiet. Fifty of the Eighty were up here on the upper floor. Fifty people snoring, wheezing, whispering, rolling over on creaky bedsprings.

Jobs pulled off his blanket and rolled over the side. Now that he was awake he had to pee. He dropped to the floor, crouched, hoping he hadn't awakened anyone. The dilemma was whether he should root around under his dad's bunk to find his shoes. If he did he might wake his parents. If he didn't he might step on one of the cockroaches.

They had very big cockroaches here in Florida.

There was more to worry about than roaches, he told himself. He crept away on bare feet, and now he passed the source of the whimpering. It was a kid he'd met in passing, a kid named Bobby or maybe Billy. Billy Weir, that was it. The kid was his own age, more or less, but seemed younger somehow.

Jobs padded by, trying to shut out the distress sounds of Billy's nightmare. Across the cracked linoleum, tensed for foot-on-roach contact, he slid through the door into the bathroom — a military-style latrine with something like a dozen ancient toilets facing a matching dozen sinks, all under the blinding, unnatural glow of fluorescent overheads. A blanket had been hung halfway down the room as a vague barrier between men's and women's rooms.

Jobs did what he had to do and was washing his hands when Billy Weir came in. Jobs gave him a civil, neutral nod; after all, guys didn't chat in the rest room. But Billy made no acknowledgment. He just stood there in bare feet, boxer shorts, and Dallas Cowboys T-shirt.

Jobs started to walk away, but it was just too strange. The boy was standing, staring, but seeing nothing.

"Must be sleepwalking," Jobs muttered out loud, comforting himself by the sound of his own voice. Billy Weir was creeping him out.

What was the deal with sleepwalkers? You weren't supposed to wake them up, or you were, or it didn't matter? Jobs couldn't remember.

Suddenly Billy started talking again in a language Jobs had surely never heard: It wasn't English or Spanish or anything like either of them. It was the voice he'd heard earlier.

"I'll get your parents, that's what I'll do," Jobs said. The hairs on the back of his neck were standing up.

"You'll be there," Billy said in clear, unaccented English.

"You awake now?"

"You'll be there. You'll be there," Billy repeated.

"Where?"

"The world . . . the creation . . . the beautiful, terrible place . . ."

"You know what? I'm just going to get your father."

"He dies. She dies. Many die. Others . . ." The boy shrugged.

"Are you awake or what?" Jobs demanded, frustration getting the better of him. "If you're awake let's cut the spook show, okay?"

Billy Weir stretched out his hand, feeling ahead

of him like a blind person, and touched Jobs's arm. He gripped the bicep, hard, almost painfully.

Jobs nearly shook him loose but was stopped cold by the expression on the boy's face. He was crying silent tears. And he looked at Jobs with sadness, but more, with deepest gratitude, like Jobs was his last friend, his savior. "You'll be there," Billy said.

CHAPTER SIXTEEN

"DON'T PANIC, BUT KEEP MOVING."

"Your attention, please. Your attention, please. Okay, folks, this is it. We have a 'go.'"

2Face stood between her mom and dad, the three of them holding hands. She felt sick. It was a sickness that went all through her. It was a feeling that permeated the room.

Until the video from San Francisco, people could avoid thinking about the details, avoid picturing what was going to happen very soon now. The death of billions was an abstraction. The death of one pretty girl at a wedding reception had driven home the reality: People would die, not billions. Friends: friends you'd had all your life, people you'd have given your last dollar. Family: your grandparents, your aunts and uncles, the cousins you played with at family reunions. All of them were going to die like that girl, like all the people in the Bay Area.

The people in the house next door, teachers, principals, coaches, the lady at the bank, the bus driver, the guys who mowed the lawn, the Starbucks girl, all the people who entertained, all those familiar faces from TV. All of them dead. Every one of them dead. Pets.

Homo sapiens, flower of evolution, lord of planet Earth. Forever dead.

The great forests, the swamps, the mountains and valleys, the deserts, obliterated. Every building, every work of art, every book, every church, obliterated.

It was too big, too awful and awe-inspiring, to fit inside your head, 2Face thought. So much waste, so much sadness, you couldn't squeeze the tiniest fraction of it into your brain.

But you could imagine being that girl, that one girl, watching the annihilation, feeling the fear, and then, the sudden knowledge that you, too, would be among the victims.

At least they would be mourned. Who would be left to mourn for the billions? Only the Eighty. The weight of that pressed down on every heart in the room.

"The buses are outside. It's about a ten-minute

ride to the launch pad. When we get there we'll un-load and call the roll to make sure everyone is there."

"It's a sick joke, just a sick joke," a man muttered behind 2Face.

2Face leaned close to her dad. "They were sup-posed to do a practice run this morning. I don't know what to do."

"I know, honey. I know. I don't know what hap-pened to the practice run."

2Face knew: San Francisco. It had gutted the staff. Some of the Marines had run off, the cooks in the mess tent, drivers, NASA techs, even the two Secret Service agents assigned to that jerk Yago.

The Eighty had been waiting for this moment for most of two days. Waiting and waiting with nothing else to do. And yet, it was too sudden. It was all too sudden. It couldn't really be happening, not right now, right now.

They shuffled down the stairs and merged with the herd of people down there. People were carry-ing their possessions, their few small things.

"Folks, if it won't fit in a pocket, it ain't going," a weirdly cheerful woman with a clipboard chirped. "Put it in the trash barrel. Don't worry, the Lord will provide, the Lord will provide. We'll have all we need in the Kingdom."

2Face stuffed a few hard-copy photos in her pockets, and her mini-book: The tiny screen was hard to read but it contained the full text of sixteen books.

"Like I'll be reading them on the flight," she muttered, almost amused at the strangeness of it all. A flight? To where? To what airport? How far? What time zone? How many hours, how many days, weeks, months, years? Centuries?

In two hours she would be in hibernation. Two hours. Would there be a time to say good-bye? Was now the time?

"Mom and Dad? I love you both," 2Face said, her throat closing up, choking off the words.

"We love you, honey," her mom said.

Her dad said nothing, just wiped his tears with the back of his hand.

The crowd was in a strange mood, or several strange moods. Many wept. Some joked, displays of bravado. Some prayed. Someone started to sing "God Bless America," but no one joined in and the tune petered out. America was just another dinosaur now.

Boarding the buses was a debacle. No one knew if buses were assigned or whether it was first come, first served. No one wanted to be separated from loved ones. People clutched precious mementos that had to be pried from their hands by touchingly patient Marines.

2Face noticed the young, black woman sergeant reasoning with a man who would not release a big stuffed lion. It had belonged to a daughter who died in infancy. His wife at last pulled the toy away from him, forceful but wailing all the while, and handed it to the sergeant. The man squeezed his arms together, squeezed emptiness and cried.

At last everyone was loaded. The buses, all full, rolled away toward the launch pad. And now silence fell. The only sound was the symphony of squeaks from the seats, the wheezing of the engines, the metallic rattle.

No one spoke. People held hands. Their lips moved, but silently. They stared around, out the windows. 2Face stared. Shadows of trees. Plants. Grass. Earth.

The shuttle was visible from miles away. It was lit up, as garish as a gas station at night. It looked like a jumbo jet strapped onto a pair of spindly rockets and an odd, outsized, rust-red fuel tank bigger than the orbiter itself. This jury-rigged craft seemed then to have been leaned against what might have been a gravel factory.

Most, if not all Americans had seen shuttle launches on TV, and at some level this massive machine seemed almost commonplace to 2Face. The tower, that maze of I-beams and platforms, was familiar as well.

In fact, the image was so commonplace that the changes stood out glaringly: big, lumpish pods placed atop the wings, an array of what might have almost been propane tanks welded down the sides, obscuring the big red, white, and blue flag and the black letters that spelled out *United States*.

At the best of times the space shuttle looked like something put together out of spare parts. Now it seemed positively trashy. A vast piece of junk, all lit up by spotlights, blotting out the stars. They had chiseled away most of the heat tiles: no need. There would be no reentry.

The sight extinguished what small shred of optimism 2Face had clung to. This was a joke. It really was a joke. No sane person would have climbed into a car that looked half this junked.

Making matters worse still, the payload door was open a crack. A ten-foot crack. From the tower a rickety catwalk extended around and through the crack, into the payload bay.

Within the payload bay it was just possible to see the steel tube grandiosely named the *Mayflower*. The tube, the *Mayflower*, was the color of lead. For a very good reason: It was sheathed in lead, some protection at least against insidious radiation.

The *Mayflower* was thirty-nine-and-a-half feet long, which took up most of the sixty-foot-long payload bay. The rest of the space was crammed with experimental oxygen generators, nutrient pumps, and the machinery of the hibernation equipment.

All together, and with the pods attached to the exterior of the orbiter, it weighed more than forty-six tons. Sixteen tons beyond the nominal lift capacity of the shuttle rockets.

The Eighty were marshaled into lines by Marines and nervous or sullen or sardonic NASA people. The weeping was mostly over now. People were awed by the towering beast above them, or depressed, or simply wondering how long it would take to load everyone aboard.

At first 2Face didn't notice the popping sounds. There was all kinds of noise around; in fact there was a steady background roar. But the Marines noticed.

They stiffened at the sound and all looked away to the south. 2Face followed the direction of their gaze and saw flashes of light.

"Gunfire," Mo'Steel said, just behind 2Face in line. "People shooting down there."

"Why?" 2Face wondered. A stupid question. She knew why. Or thought she did.

Mo'Steel looked surprised. "They want to climb on board the big ride, 'miga. This is the big woolly. Nothing woollier. Three g's on top of a monster firecracker."

"You think they're looking for thrills?" she asked, a bit incredulous.

Mo'Steel frowned thoughtfully. "Or maybe they're just thinking it would save their lives, or whatever."

Suddenly, there was new shooting, and much closer. Out of the darkness a pair of vehicles raced, engines roaring. Trucks? Humvees? Three hundred yards away, no more.

BamBamBamBam!

"Everybody down!" a voice cried.

2Face dropped, hurt her knees on the tarmac, crouched, trying to see what was happening.

Automatic-weapon fire blazed from the approaching vehicles. Someone cried out in surprise.

2Face saw a large man stand up and pull his shirt open to see the red stains, the hole in his belly. He took a stagger step and fell.

"Oh, oh, nooo!" a woman's voice cried. "Someone help! My husband's been shot."

2Face saw the strange kid named Billy Weir. He was standing there, standing as if he was unaware of the bullets, or indifferent.

2Face stared, her attention riveted. The man near the boy had been shot. And the boy was standing, arms at his side, doing nothing, saying nothing.

"Get down, you idiot!" someone yelled and dragged Billy down. That broke the spell and 2Face tore her gaze away.

The Marines were returning fire. They were on one knee, aiming carefully, blazing away. Controlled bursts of shattering noise.

Sergeant Tamara Hoyle was yelling orders and firing her own weapon. Suddenly a muffled explosion and an eruption of yellow flames in the night. The humvee spun, teetered as if it would turn over, righted itself and stopped. It burned furiously.

2Face saw a man running from the vehicle. He was on fire. 2Face screamed, screamed, the sound coming from deep within, a sound torn from memories of pain. Her mother grabbed her, held her tight.

A Marine shot the burning man and he fell.

The Eighty were all down now, crawling or just hugging the tarmac as the firefight went on over their heads. Bullets were everywhere.

The second vehicle was still coming on. It, too, was on fire now, but still coming. The violence of the noise was stunning. Hundreds of rounds, all so near. A ricochet. A soft *thunpf!* as a bullet buried itself in the soft tarmac by 2Face's arm.

An explosion, louder than the first. This time 2Face felt the concussion, the wave of superheated air.

"Cease firing, cease firing!" Tamara Hoyle yelled. "Weller, that means you!"

2Face raised her head a few inches. The second vehicle was stopped, no more than a few feet from the cowering civilians. Flashlights played over its bullet-pocked sheet metal. A body hung grotesquely out of the driver's side window.

2Face saw Tamara Hoyle motion two of her men forward. They ran to the vehicle. One of them fired twice.

Pop! Pop!

Then, "All secure here."

"My husband!" the woman cried, still. "Oh, my God, oh no, oh no."

"Everyone up!" the sergeant commanded. "There could be more coming. No running! Don't panic, but keep moving. Keep moving."

2Face got up, helped her mom to stand.

She stepped past the body of the dead man, tried not to look, tried not to hear his wife's heartbroken keening.

Tried not to imagine seven billion more just as dead.

CHAPTER SEVENTEEN

"THEY'RE ON THEIR WAY HERE, WELL-ARMED, CRAZY, NOTHING TO LOSE."

It was never going to be smooth, Yago knew that going in. It was too rushed. Too hurried. The whole crazy enterprise had always had a strong smell of desperation about it.

But after the shooting, the blazing guns in the darkness, with more out in the distance, now it was borderline panic.

At least the weeping had stopped. Funny how no one was moaning about what a waste of time the whole thing was. No. Once someone tries to take life away from you, that's when you really start to care about it.

But, that cynical insight aside, Yago was deeply unhappy. Unhappiness expressed itself as anger.

"What kind of idiot is responsible for security here?" he demanded loudly of no one in particular.

He focused his rage on the sergeant. "You. How hard is it to stop some ignorant idiots in a pickup truck? I could have been hurt."

"You still could be," she snarled. "Now move along."

"Are you threatening me?"

"No. Just stating facts. There's a full-fledged riot going on in half the cities in the country right now. The mother of all riots is at the gates. They're on their way here, well-armed, crazy, nothing to lose."

"Well, stop them!" Yago shrilled.

Some others had stopped to listen to this news. There was scared murmuring, and, to Yago's distinct pleasure, a vague support for him.

"There are Marines and airmen out there dying to do just that," Tamara answered, jerking her head toward the not-so-distant sounds of gunfire. "And just so you know: There are others that have changed sides. You got soldiers shooting soldiers out there, and I don't know who is going to win. So maybe you'd better move it."

Yago knew better than to prolong the argument. "All right, everyone, let's go," he proclaimed, assuming a mantle of authority.

There was a crush of bodies around the single open-cage elevator ascending the tower. It was definitely intimidating, standing down here almost directly beneath the huge inverted funnels of the rocket engines. Once they lit the fuse anyone still down here would be a pork rind.

Yago shouldered ahead and managed to squeeze aboard the next elevator.

Up and up. Up past the disconcerting sight of workmen still using arc welders. They were still working on the shuttle. Using welders despite the fact that the fuel was loaded. Taking terrible risks that spoke of terrible necessity.

Up and up. The elevator jerked to a stop and the gate rattled open. White-coated NASA techs were waiting to usher them out onto a windy platform. Yago looked over the edge. Twelve, fifteen stories or so to the ground.

From up here he could clearly see the muzzle flashes of the battle. Closer. Still maybe a mile away, but a mile was a minute to a person in a humvee.

"Okay, listen up," a white-coated NASA man said in a slurred voice. *Was he drunk?* Yago wondered. He was! The man was drunk.

"You just walk out, one at a time, along the catwalk. Someone's waiting inside to stow you in your berth. One at a time. Nothing to it."

Yago watched as the first person stepped out.

The catwalk swayed in the warm, moist wind, and swayed some more with each step. The catwalk went out, turned a dog-leg, and disappeared inside the partly open payload bay.

More went. Some with easy, confident strides. Others hesitant. One by one.

The elevator arrived with another load. The last load. The Marine sergeant and half a dozen of her men joined. They lined the rickety platform, weapons aimed downward.

A kid, some kid Yago hadn't noticed before, started to freak out. He didn't want to go out onto the catwalk.

"I'm scared," he whispered to his parents, and clung to them.

"Go on, you baby," Yago snapped. "What are you, three years old? Get out there."

"He's always been scared of heights," his mother said pitifully to the anxious faces around her. "Sweetheart, you can do it. Just hold onto the rails and take it one step at a time."

But the kid wasn't buying. "It'll break. The whole thing will break."

"Hey, Little Big Man, don't sweat it." It was Mo'Steel. "Watch this."

Mo'Steel took a hop, landed on his hands, and

proceeded to walk out onto the catwalk. He turned around, gave the kid an upside-down grin, then executed a gasp-inducing move that involved leaping up onto the rickety railing itself and tight-rope walking.

Someone, presumably the lunatic's father, bellowed at him to get down, get off of there!

Mo'Steel hopped back down onto the catwalk and grinned at the scared kid. "Nothing to it, Little Big: You and me."

"Supposed to be just one at a time," the kid argued.

"Hey, it breaks I'll catch it and tie it off onto the whole rocket up there."

Somehow Mo'Steel's infectious, confident idiocy (as Yago saw it) worked. Mo'Steel held out his hand and the boy took it.

Yago stewed. Should have just pushed the kid aside. Little creep. And that overgrown monkey showing off like that? Of course, he was on the list already for having knocked Yago down. Now he was on the list with a star by his name.

Across the catwalk. Out over a very long drop. Yago was halfway across when a siren loud enough to break glass erupted at full, fearsome volume. Yago nearly jumped off.

The welders, the workmen, everyone on the

tower, all dropped tools and ran for it. Yago could see white coats flooding away, down below, rats scurrying to waiting buses and trucks.

"They're just clearing the blast zone," someone explained.

Why bother? Yago wondered. *Fry now, fry later.*

Yago kept moving. Into the payload bay, face-to-face now with the big lead cylinder. It looked way too much like a stylized coffin. There was a door-sized opening in it, a hatch. Yago stepped through and was handed along by a NASA person. This one was sober, at least.

Through the hatch, and now it was no longer a fear of heights that was a problem, but claustrophobia. Yago had always hated confined spaces. His nightmares were of closed spaces. Being locked in a box, unable to escape.

The inside of the *Mayflower* was about as cramped as the belowdecks of the original *Mayflower.* It was all garishly lit, but the light only seemed to accentuate the close nature of it.

The pod, the *Mayflower,* had been built on thirteen levels, with six berths per level. Seventy-eight berths in all, crammed into a space just thirty-six-feet tall by twelve feet wide. Each of the thirteen "decks" was little more than a strengthened wire shelf. A tiny, winding stairway led up and down through the levels.

Down, just below him, through the wire mesh, Yago could see faces looking up at him from within their berths.

Coffins. The berths were nothing but Plexiglas-topped coffins. Scared faces stared up at him through the glass, scared, buried alive.

Yago felt the panic grab him. His legs went rubbery.

"Move along," the NASA tech said. "Climb up. All full below."

Somehow Yago made his legs move. Somehow he climbed the ludicrously small stairway. Another white coat was waiting, straddling the stair and deck.

"In here. You have to crawl across. Come on, keep moving."

Yago wanted to vomit. Impossible. He was shaking, could anyone see? Did they know? Had to keep moving, couldn't lose it, couldn't lose it.

He clambered across one empty berth and dropped into the one indicated for him. Number fifty-one. Was that any kind of omen? What did the number mean? He should have been number one.

It was narrow, well-padded. Long enough for a

six-foot-tall man, but so narrow it pressed against Yago's shoulders.

He lay there, looking up at the deck above him, looking up at the bottom of another berth, less than a foot and a half from his own nose. Looking longingly at the small empty space between berths, clinging to that miniscule bit of open space.

The lid slid closed without warning. Plastic, inches from his nose.

"Don't cry," he told himself. "Whatever you do, *do not* cry."

CHAPTER EIGHTEEN

"WE'RE GOING TO GO AHEAD AND LIGHT THE CANDLE."

Jobs and his parents were the last to board. They climbed to the highest level. He passed Mo'Steel in berth sixty-two. His friend gave him a wink and said, "Hey, Duck, you finally going to catch some rush with me, huh?"

"Looks like it, Mo," Jobs said. The lid slid closed over his friend's face. Mo'Steel made a mock-scared face.

Up and up, past genuinely scared faces, weeping faces, and always sadness. Beneath any other emotion, deepest sadness.

"Or maybe that's just me," he whispered under his breath. The image of Cordelia, the last image of her, that horrible vision, was never far from his mind. He had known her in a confession, in a kiss, in memory. But somehow what was real and personal had been superseded by pictures, the ones she had taken. Organic memories overwritten by digital memories. He had to strain to focus on the true memory of her lips on his, and that memory was too painful to reach for.

He ascended and crawled to one of the outboard berths. Above him another mesh deck, but more open. Up there on the final, roomier level were just two berths, flanked by racks that held two rumpled white space suits. Spares, presumably, for the crew. The flight deck was just above, through a tiny hatch. Up there the pilot and copilot were going through a rushed checklist, readying what would be the final shuttle flight.

Jobs had never thought of himself as claustrophobic, but he was glad to be next to the stairs. He had more of a sense of room, more open space, more to "look at" than just about anyone. He lay on his back, said, "Kind of tight, huh?" to his dad. And, "You okay, Mom?"

Then, from the corner of his eye, he could have sworn he saw one of the racked space suits move.

Surely not. Someone else would have noticed, too. But no, no, he was the only one at the right angle to see.

The Plexiglas lid closed over him, catching him by surprise. There were speakers inside the berth, but no microphone. Just like that he'd been shut off from the outside world. The speakers gave instructions in a neutral, computer-generated voice.

"Please locate the blue tube pinned to the right side of the berth, and pull the end piece toward you."

Jobs could just raise his head high enough to look down at his feet. He found the tube and pulled it toward him.

"Place the end of the tube in the back of your throat. The coated capsule on the end of the tube will make swallowing painless and easy. Now swallow the capsule and, using your hands, slowly and gently push the tube down until the red band reaches your mouth. Please take care not to vomit."

"Sure, no problem," Jobs grated. He swallowed, like swallowing a very large vitamin tablet. But the tube made his gorge rise. He waited till he was past it. Pushed some more. Gross. A horrible feeling.

"Now draw the transparent plastic helmet over your head, taking care not to tangle the breathing tube."

This was like sticking your head in a balloon. The plastic was malleable, creepily soft. It stuck to his forehead and pressed down on his eyes, making it hard to keep them open. He adjusted it as well as he could, but it pulled painfully on his hair.

He took a tentative breath. Strange-smelling air. Metallic.

He could feel his heart pounding. Feel the blood rushing through the veins in his neck.

Another voice. Human, this time. "Folks, this is Colonel Jasper Willett, the mission commander. You were supposed to get training for all this, folks, dry runs and so on. I know this isn't easy, any of it. But try and follow the computer directions as well as you can. They'll be repeated."

Jobs worked again to adjust the smothering helmet to something like comfort.

Outside the berth the Marine sergeant loomed into view, making a final check. He felt an acute stab of guilt. She had defended them at risk of her own life. Now she would be left behind. She would die when the Rock slammed into Earth. If not sooner.

Jobs wondered how many people would take their own lives before the end. Would the sergeant wait patiently somewhere, find a place to sip a last cold drink, maybe say a prayer, be with a special loved one?

The sergeant looked around, met Jobs's gaze, and actually managed a smile and a thumbs-up.

Things happened very quickly then. One of the space suits moved, just a bit. Tamara Hoyle spun, leveled her weapon, and yelled something Jobs couldn't hear.

Her back was to the other suit. A gun appeared, raised in ghostly style by the white suit, held by the rubber-tipped glove. Someone inside, invisible behind the gold-coated sun shield of the helmet.

Jobs yelled, "Look out!"

He saw a flash. Heard only a distant explosion. Saw Tamara Hoyle spin and fire all in one easy move. Three holes appeared in the space suit. No blood visible, but the suit sagged.

Tamara Hoyle clutched at her shoulder. She pulled her hand away, saw blood.

The speaker crackled. "Okay, folks, we've just got the word to cut short the prep. We got some bad guys outside, getting a little too close for comfort. We're going to go ahead and light the candle." Commander Willett was trying to maintain the inevitably laconic NASA tone, but he was clearly worried. "Anyone on board who isn't berthed needs to exit immediately and get into one of the blast-shelters. And I mean right now."

Tamara Hoyle started to climb down the ladder but she seemed unable to make her arm work properly. Jobs saw her frown.

Didn't they know she was still on board? Did

they know? Someone had to help her. Someone had to help her.

Tamara collapsed, all at once, fell onto her back on the deck, head jammed between two berths, legs hanging down the steps. She was almost directly over Jobs's head. A red splat landed on the plastic lid, like a raindrop.

Tamara lay staring up, mad at herself for being caught off-guard. Mad at herself for letting a little bullet stop her. It didn't hurt all that much, that was strange. She felt the deck vibrating beneath her. Saw the space suit she'd shot. Someone in there. And someone in the other suit, too. The other suit was moving, looking like a marionette worked by a distracted puppeteer. Awkward. Like whoever was in it was trying to get out, or at least get off the hook that held the suit secure.

D-Caf was trying both. His feet were off the deck, couldn't move. Couldn't go to his brother. "Mark! Mark!" he cried. "Mark!"

He writhed, unable to do anything but hang there. Everything was dark, shaded through the suit's visor. He saw three holes in his brother's suit. Maybe the bullets had missed. Maybe. It was possible, wasn't it?

But they surely had not missed the soldier. She lay there breathing heavily, unable to move.

And now the rumbling of the ship grew very suddenly.

Far below, the fire was lit. It exploded downward and outward and billowed up in a geyser of flame and smoke.

The rioters had made it through the determined resistance. They reached the launch pad just as the rocket fuel and liquid oxygen came together to explode in a blowtorch of incomprehensible energy.

The rioters turned and ran, turned their vehicles around. Far too late.

Superheated gas billowed yellow and orange. It incinerated the rioters in a heartbeat. It reduced the vehicles to tin shells.

The tired, overburdened old space shuttle carrying the Mayflower mission lifted up from the pad.

CHAPTER NINETEEN

"YOU'RE WEIGHTLESS, YOU IDIOT."

Numbness spread outward, radiating out from the hole in Tamara Hoyle's shoulder. Couldn't feel one side of her neck. Couldn't feel her arm. Her brain, too, seemed numb, vague, wandering. And now something huge was sitting on her chest, pressing her down. An elephant on her chest.

The baby, the baby, the baby. God let the baby be okay.

Tamara couldn't breathe. Couldn't raise her head. She was being shaken, vibrated. A roar in her ears. There was blood in her eyes, darkness blurring her vision. She saw the space suit she'd shot. It hung low, the three g's were weighing it down.

She turned her head, a slow, slow movement. The other suit, writhing, but sluggishly. The violence of liftoff made everything blur, like someone holding a jerky video camera. Things left trails. Hallucinatory.

Her legs were dangling down the stairwell and now the deck was tilting sharply. She would slide down, was sliding, slipping. It would kill her. A three-gravity fall was not good.

She still had her weapon, felt it in the one hand that could still feel. Had to wedge it. Had to jam it into the wire mesh, use it to hold on.

But the deck was tilting further still, way over, like a pitched roof. And she was weak. Slow. Fuzzy.

The gun was torn slowly, inexorably from her hand. Her strong grip not strong enough. Slipping and sliding on her own blood.

She fell, an eruption of stars in her head, and she lay where she fell, crumpled and jammed into a ball.

Jobs banged on the top of his berth. It was like he was lifting weights with each move. Had he been the only one to see? He was at an angle, maybe so, maybe no one else knew. Maybe it was up to him, him and no one else. He couldn't see what had happened to the Marine. He could see the other suit, though, the terrorist or whatever he was.

The lid didn't open. Inside release? Surely they'd built in a panic-button? A release? They wouldn't lock people into these things with no way to get out.

But now there was something else happening. Weird. Like when he had his appendix taken out and they'd given him anesthesia. That's what it felt like, only slow, very slow-working. The hibernation technology was beginning to work. He was being drawn under, down into a state that would be far, far deeper than sleep.

He scrabbled around, searching with lead fingers, unable to turn his head far enough to see around inside the berth. Oh, man, so sleepy. Where was the release? Where . . .

Where would you put it, Jobs? he asked himself silently. *Come on, man, where would it have to be?*

Should be an easy engineering question. Easy. Unless your brain was being shut down.

D-Caf could see him. He could see the kid in the nearest berth on the deck below, seemingly panicking, pushing, trying to get out. It only added to D-Caf's own panic. Mark had been shot and now he was trapped. The g's were draining the blood out of his head. His feet ached and buzzed. His head was woozy, dreamy, scared, unable to focus, inchoate panic. Had to get out. Mark. Help him.

The ship was tilted over, D-Caf was on his back

now, less straight downward pressure, and now he got his heels into a seam and kicked. The suit jerked up and out of its rack. He slid down the wall and slammed way too hard into the pitched deck. His knees buckled. The wind was knocked out of him. But his brain was clearing a little. A little, not much.

D-Caf crawled uphill, more and more uphill toward Mark. Crawled through blood. He clawed his way to his brother, weeping inside his helmet, crying, "Mark! Mark!"

And then, quite suddenly, the ceaseless roar stopped. Not silence, but near silence, comparative silence.

And all at once he could move quite easily. Too easily. He smacked his helmet into a bulkhead.

"Weightless. I'm weightless, Mark," he said.

He pulled himself cautiously up to be level with Mark. How did you open these stupid helmets? The ring. Okay, yeah, he could do it.

D-Caf removed his brother's helmet, talking to him all the while. The helmet came off. A lava lamp of blood bubbled up from inside.

Mark was slumped down inside. Dead. Dead beyond any illusion.

D-Caf cried out. He shoved back and floated across the space, slammed into one of the unused berths and bounced upward to slam against the now-overhead bulkhead.

What was he going to do? What was he supposed to do now? Mark was dead. And the two empty berths they were going to take away from the pilot . . . The pilots were still alive. That was the problem. They were still alive.

D-Caf was alone, completely alone now. What was he supposed to do? No Mark. No Mark to make the decision.

The gun, Mark's gun, their father's gun was hanging suspended in midair.

D-Caf reached for it.

He heard a noise, an exhaust sound, air rushing.

He slapped the bulkhead and spun around. He caught the gun, fumbled it, grabbed for it, just as Jobs came flying too fast, too hard up out of his berth, up the stairwell.

Jobs had meant to hit the terrorist, because terrorist he surely was, with his shoulder but caught him only a glancing blow. He stuck out his hand, grabbed the gunman, spun him around, and then himself hit the far bulkhead.

The impact stunned him. There was a shocking jolt of pain in his head and neck.

"You're weightless, you idiot," he scolded himself, "not massless." In the middle of it all, fighting an armed bad guy, he still felt a stab of embarrassment at mishandling weightlessness.

Jobs flattened against the bulkhead as well as he could, and now pushed off with much less force. He drifted, spread-eagle. The gunman was spinning in midair, just like a top, maybe twenty rpm's. Every three seconds or so the gun came around.

Jobs drifted. The gunman came around.

Bam!

Flame shot from the muzzle. It canceled D-Caf's rotation, but knocked him slowly backward. Jobs was helpless, still floating, nothing within reach, slowly descending on D-Caf, who now leveled the gun.

The hatch opened. A space-suited astronaut stuck his head in. The gunman jerked, wavered, as if uncertain who to point the gun at.

Jobs stretched with all his might and just tapped a passing support beam. Now his drift was a spin. He could hear a muffled, faraway voice yelling. Something. Yelling, yelling.

The astronaut slid into the room, held his hands up in a placating gesture.

The terrorist fired.

The faceplate of the astronaut's helmet cracked

like safety glass. Jobs was upside down now. He kicked at the overhead and hit the gunman from above and behind.

The gun flew and banged loudly around. The terrorist slammed into the deck with Jobs now clinging to him, a monkey on his back.

The gunman was yelling, yelling, and now, in direct contact, Jobs could understand. "It's a mistake! It's a mistake! I didn't mean to shoot! I didn't mean to shoot!"

A kid's voice! Just the same, whoever he was, he was writhing, squirming, trying to throw off his tackler. But the suit was far too big for him. It was like trying to fight from inside a big canvas bag.

And all at once there was another set of powerful arms added to the struggle. The other astronaut. Jobs caught a flash of the name stenciled on his suit: COL. J.W. WILLETT.

Between them the commander and Jobs pried off the helmet. The two of them blinked in surprise.

"I didn't mean to do it," the kid cried. "I didn't want to hurt anyone."

"You shot him in the face, you lying little —" Jobs yelled. "You shot him!"

"I was scared, I didn't mean to shoot!"

A floating balloon of blood splashed greasily across the young killer's face. The copilot's, the Marine's, or the other bad guy's, no way to know.

The commander left the sobbing kid in Jobs's hands and went to check on his copilot. When he came back his face was dark and murderous.

"He's dead," he grated.

Jobs noticed a hole in the commander's right hand. Stray bullet? "They shot someone else, too," Jobs said. "The Marine. The sergeant, I think she was. I don't know what happened to her. This guy was in one suit, someone else was in the other suit. It was the other guy who shot the Marine."

The commander removed his own helmet. He ripped off his gloves and looked at a round, red hole right in the center of his palm. "I have to contact Houston. I don't have authority to deal with this. There's nothing about this in the mission plan."

Jobs nodded. He was completely ready to let the commander decide. And if Colonel Willett said call Houston, that was fine.

"What's your name?" Willett demanded of the blubbering killer.

"D-Caf. It's D-Caf. You can call me Harlin if you want to, though," he answered. "That's my brother over there. Mark. Mark Melman. He wasn't trying to hurt anyone."

"You show up with a gun, you're trying to hurt someone!" Jobs snapped. "There's one, maybe two people dead. Not trying to hurt anyone?"

"It was the Rock, not us," D-Caf moaned.

"First, we get you out of that suit," Willett ordered D-Caf. "There'll be air pressure in here for the next few hours. A little less with the hole you managed to shoot in the hull. And after that you can breathe vacuum."

CHAPTER TWENTY

"GET ME HIS BERTH NUMBER.
I'LL THAW HIM OUT."

The shuttle carrying the Mayflower Project orbited Earth. Those humans below on the planet who knew about them were few. Those that cared, fewer still. Sliding across the day-night barrier into the shadow of Earth, Willett and Jobs could see the lights of a thousand cities and towns. Some were made extra bright by the raging fires of uncontrolled rioting.

The man and the boy were exhausted. They had tied D-Caf up to a support beam. They had maneuvered the unconscious but still breathing Tamara Hoyle into the berth once assigned to the man who'd died on the ground. They'd bandaged the hole in her shoulder. A Band-Aid for a bullet wound.

They had contacted Houston. Houston had said it was up to them. Houston, most of it, most of the men and women who manned the consoles and stood by at the ready, most of them had gone home to family to wait for the end.

Earth was done with the *Mayflower*. Good luck, *Mayflower*. Leave us.

"The woman may live," Willett said. "For a while, anyway. At least we got the tube in her. Maybe the hibernation will help somehow. I don't know what to do with the kid."

Jobs shrugged. He didn't know, either.

"One thing I know: I'm not a jury or a judge," the astronaut said.

"No," Jobs agreed.

"I'll put him in Tom's berth. Not that it matters much. See this?" He pointed to a readout on the overhead console.

Jobs had been surveying the cockpit with some interest. It was his kind of place: hundreds of knobs and dials and LED readouts.

"That's the solar sails."

"The readout's blank," Jobs said.

"Yeah. Nothing. No feedback. Could be the readout is just malfunctioning. Could be the processor. Could be a software glitch. My guess? Wire's been severed. Which means they don't deploy. Which means we drift out of this solar system of ours at a very leisurely pace."

"Solar sails?"

Willett nodded. "Yeah. Microthin sheets of some new composite. Supposed to be incredibly strong. And supposedly more efficient, much more efficient. When they were first looking at solar sails as a means of propulsion, most guesses were they'd give us 150,000 miles per hour maximum before we left the solar system. But these are supposed to be different. Don't ask me how."

"What kind of speed can we achieve with these new sails?"

"The contractor claims we can loop around the sun and come out the other side doing just under a million miles per hour. Pretty slow, still, considering you're using light for your wind and the light is moving 186,000 miles per second. And pretty slow if you're talking about traveling light-years through space. But better than orbital speed by a long shot. Of course, that's if they were spread. And right now they're snug in their pods and not going anywhere."

"Isn't there some way to fix them?"

Willett smiled. "The standard NASA answer is 'can do.' But NASA . . . Well, they hung in there pretty good, you know. They stuck it out till we were off. But they have wives and husbands. They got kids and grandkids they want to spend their last hours with."

"Yeah."

For a long while neither of them spoke. Through the windows Jobs could see the sun come up, peeking around the rim of the planet. Daylight somewhere over West Africa. Sunrise, but everyone onboard was fast, fast asleep. They were the only two people awake, aside from D-Caf.

Then Willett said, "We would need an EVA. Someone would have to go out there and literally pry open those pods. There's supposed to be a manual release there. Supposed to be a crank you can turn, cranks 'em right out. So they tell me."

Jobs said, "Maybe we should try that."

Willett held up his bandaged hand.

Jobs held up his own hand. "I could do it."

"It's a two-man job. Worse than that, it's a tight space, no room. You're small enough, maybe, but we'd need a second man, small as you."

"I have a friend," Jobs said.

Willett looked intrigued. "Would he do it? Go outside, I mean?"

Jobs smiled. "If I didn't take him he'd kill me."

Willett hesitated. Then, "Get me his berth number. I'll thaw him out."

CHAPTER TWENTY-ONE

"THAT'S THE ROCK."

"Mo. Wake up."

Mo'Steel opened one eye. Then the other. Jobs was leaning right over him. "Are we there?"

Jobs shook his head. "No. You've only been under for a couple hours."

"Huh." He snorted, rubbed his nose, and sat up. "What's it about, Duck?"

"Bad stuff, Mo. People getting shot. Some crazy kid and his big brother got in, shot that Marine sergeant."

"That hot-looking black fem?"

Jobs cocked an eyebrow. "I didn't really think about whether she was hot, Mo."

"Mmm. You wouldn't. So things are screwed up and we're gonna auger into the sun or whatever and you woke me up so I wouldn't miss it?"

"Kind of. Here's the thing: One of the pilots is dead. The other is injured. Some kind of solar sails or whatever won't deploy. Unless someone goes outside."

Mo'Steel blinked. Then his eyes lit up. "Outside? Ride the big rocket from the outside?"

For a moment Jobs thought his friend might cry. Mo'Steel grabbed his arm and squeezed. "You're the *best,* man."

"The commander wanted to know if you'd do it. It's dangerous. Very dangerous. The suits won't fit us, the jetpacks are hard to control, we screw up at all and we could end up being separated from the ship. That'd mean we'd probably orbit till we entered the atmosphere and burned up."

Mo'Steel sat bolt upright. "Let's go!"

"You're a dangerously disturbed person, Mo. But one more thing before you say yes: the Rock. It's coming. We have a very small window for an escape burn to push us out of orbit. The calculations are all based on the sails being deployed before the burn. Colonel Willett may have to light the rockets while we're still out there."

"Very woolly," Mo'Steel agreed, nodding with approval, as though this particular ride had been worked out just for his amusement. "Hey! We're weightless."

"Yes. You can thank me later."

They suited up as quickly as they could with

one-armed help from Willett. Slipping into a suit to hide as D-Caf had done was one thing. Actually donning the suit properly so that it would work out in the vacuum of space was another.

Willett walked them through the procedure as well as he could while simultaneously prepping the ship for a burn with his one good hand. Jobs noticed that he had Mark's revolver on his lap. Jobs wondered how many rounds were left.

"You'll need to loosen all the bolts holding the sheathing in place. Cast the sheath off. This is important: Don't throw it forward or back, throw it away from the ship." He made a motion with both hands and winced at the pain. "And remember your basic physics: equal and opposite reaction, right?"

"Under the sheathing you'll find the sails coiled up. It'll look like a big wad of Mylar. Crumpled-up foil. Supposedly this stuff, though, has a shape memory. Meaning, once you crank the 'mast' all the way out, the sail should snap into place and spread out on its own. Should. No one's ever tested this. Like I told you, the calculations — such as they are — call for the sails to be fully deployed prior to escaping orbit. I don't know how critical that is. Figure we should do our best."

Mo'Steel nodded. "Don't worry, Captain. My boy's got the tech chops."

Willett looked at Jobs with a flicker more interest. "Steven Jobs, huh? That's the name you chose? Not Gates or Boole or Eckert or Shastri?"

Jobs smiled. "Steve Jobs made a revolution in a garage."

"Fair enough," Willett said with a sigh. "One of my own boys is pretty good at . . ." He fell silent. He glanced at the revolver. "Okay. I punch up the burn in twenty-five minutes. The Rock . . . it's going to happen soon. I'll call you in at the five-minute point. That's just maybe enough time to get into the airlock and brace yourself."

"Mmmm." Mo'Steel rocked back and forth on the balls of his feet, anticipating the rush.

No time for more. No time for anything like the usual NASA care and caution and endless preparation.

Jobs caught sight of a small framed picture wedged into one of the control panels. It showed a middle-aged woman, a girl, and two boys, all in their early twenties or late teens.

He wondered if he should say something. But here, now, more than at any time in his life, Jobs found the right words would not come. He wondered if he should take the gun. But how could he explain it?

Watching a wreck, watching a slow-motion disaster, unable to do anything, anything at all to stop it. Unable even to think of comforting words. Powerless . . .

Jobs turned away. Mo'Steel slapped his shoulder, oblivious, of course, to his friend's particular concern.

They sealed each other's helmets and stepped into the miniscule airlock. Waited while the air was sucked away, drawn back into the ship.

The indicator light was green.

Mo'Steel threw the latch and levered the hatch open.

Earth was right there, right there, filling the frame. Mo'Steel pushed off very slowly and drifted up through the hatch, or down through the hatch, or left or right or whatever. *It was all the same,* he thought happily.

He drifted through and arrested his movement by reaching down to grab the hatch threshold. He extended outward, legs pointing at Earth. He reached down to lift his friend up/down after him.

Jobs floated out into space, held Mo'Steel's hand, and they both looked back along the orbiter's back. The tall tail just touched the rim of the planet. The disorientation was extreme and impossible to resist. The ship was above, below, Earth was down or up, impossible.

Hard not to feel like that big old ball, that blue and green and brown ball in the black sky was going to fall on them and crush them. At the same time, it was hard not to feel like you were falling, like you ought to be screaming.

It was impossible to make any sense of it. At least it would be to Jobs, Mo'Steel realized. Funny how you could see tension even through a space suit. It was the way Jobs held himself, all clenched up. Clenched up and hanging upside down above the big ball.

"Don't think it, Duck," he advised. "Gotta just do, not think. Follow me."

Jobs closed his eyes, tried to dispel the sense that he was falling. Opened his eyes again, and this time narrowed his gaze, focused on his friend. This was Mo's thing, follow Mo.

Mo'Steel held Jobs's shoulder, got behind him, and keyed his maneuvering jets. The two of them eased forward, Jobs balanced like a clumsy but insignificant weight.

They flew at a snail's pace. Willett had emphasized conserving the maneuvering jets. So they flew very slowly above the orbiter, passing along the long, tight-closed seam of the payload bay, within which slept the Eighty, oblivious, unaware.

"There are the pods," Jobs said.

"Left or right?"

"Left."

Mo'Steel keyed his thrusters and they changed vector to intercept the pod on the left wing.

"I think I can land right on it," Jobs said and stuck his feet out.

"I don't think so, Duck. Gotta kill momentum with the jets. You'd just bounce off."

Moments later they were stopped dead — relative to the shuttle. In reality they were traveling at 18,000 miles per hour, give or take. But the elongated pod now appeared to be hanging vertically in front of them, hanging on a long, curved, white wall.

"Wrench," Jobs said. He felt more comfortable now. This was man and machine. He could do that.

"Forgot the wrench," Mo'Steel said.

"What?"

"Joke. Untie the gut-knots there, 'migo."

Jobs cursed Mo'Steel under his breath, took the wrench, and began loosening bolts. There were twelve, all around the edge of the thin sheathing. He took each bolt and stuffed them into a net bag hanging or floating from his waist.

On the seventh bolt he noticed the small round hole.

"There's what did it, there's what cut the wire. Bullet hole. Must have been a stray round from the fight on the ground."

"Hey, look," Mo'Steel said.

"What?"

"Is that it?" Mo'Steel tapped Jobs's shoulder and pointed.

Jobs looked. A small, tumbling, moving object that caught and reflected the sun's light. Small at least compared to the immensity of the planet. How could that rock possibly hurt this beautiful planet? Surely somehow it would stop, or miss, or not really do the damage everyone said.

Surely not.

People wouldn't die. No. Continents would not be shattered. No. Something would stop it, something, someone would not let it happen.

"Yeah, Mo. That's it," Jobs said. "That's the Rock."

CHAPTER TWENTY-TWO

"TWO WHOLE SECONDS TO SIT HERE AND CHAT."

They pushed the sheath away. Jobs squeezed his arm and shoulder and part of his upper body into the tight gap between the folded mast and the outer shell of the shuttle. Mo'Steel had to squeeze in beside him to hold down a latch-pawl to allow the crank to turn.

Jobs turned the small hand crank once. Twice. Almost impossible to get any kind of leverage. He was eating up time and knew it. But the gloves were bulky and way too big, the space too tight.

He turned again and again and nothing happened.

The Rock was in view. Coming. Coming. No drama, no tail of sparks, no swooshing sound. It occurred to Jobs that it was a pretty lame special effect.

The mast began to lift. Now there was more

room, and now he could get leverage, with Mo'Steel anchoring him. The crank turned quickly. The mast rose, as thin as a kid's fishing rod. The crumpled foil sail rose, too, like wadded-up tinfoil.

Up and up.

Slow. Too slow.

"Boys, this is Colonel Willett. I see you're making progress, but we're ten minutes to burn."

Jobs keyed his intercom. "Right. Almost have the left sail extended. Mo, I'm wearing out: Take a turn."

They traded places and Mo'Steel spun the crank as fast as he could. Each working till he was sweating and gasping, then handing it off. At last the crank stopped. The sail was extended.

They jetted as quickly as they could over the hump of the shuttle's back to the right wing. Removing the sheathing was easier this time.

They squeezed themselves into place and started to turn the crank.

"Gotta call time, gentlemen," Willett said. "Maybe one sail deployed is enough."

Jobs said, "Commander Willett, I'm not an astrophysicist, but aren't we talking about calculations for escaping solar orbit? I mean, we can burn our way out of Earth's orbit, but then we have to loop the sun and head out without being captured by the sun's gravity, right? If we mess with the formula we could end up in orbit forever. Or worse."

"Son, these calculations are half guesswork anyway. You have to understand, this isn't the usual NASA mission. No one knows anything for sure."

Jobs looked at Mo'Steel, caught his attention. He lifted his gold visor and pressed his helmet into contact so they could talk without using the mike and being overheard.

"Mo. I think maybe we gotta do this. But he has to fire the rockets. Maybe we can use our tethers, stay alive, hold on . . ."

"Ride the big rocket and Mother G trying to kill us real hard? You asking or telling?"

"You in?"

"What, like you're going to take a ride while I bunny?" Mo'Steel laughed, but not happily. He knew the difference between wild risks and sheer suicide. "I'll ride along with you, Jobs."

Jobs keyed his mike. "Commander, we're staying out here." He began cranking again, winding as hard and fast as he could.

"Three minutes to burn," was Willett's only answer.

Jobs and Mo'Steel cranked wildly, spelling each other every minute to keep the speed up, smooth now, practiced. The mast extended languidly. The sails grew. Not fast enough. Not fast enough.

"Two minutes," Willett said. "There's a sort of carabiner on your belts. You can clip it to the loop on your lifeline and then clip the carabiner to the sail crank itself."

"Roger that," Jobs gasped.

"Roger that?" Mo'Steel mocked. "You gone astronaut now?"

"One minute. Repeat, one minute."

The mast rose. Up and out, impossibly far, with spiderweb veins extending much farther still, extending the Mylar for thousands of square feet. Fully extended, each sail could have blanketed a pair of football fields.

"Thirty seconds."

"Let me in," Mo'Steel yelled. He grabbed the crank and worked it like a fiend.

Jobs found the carabiner and with numb fingers snapped it through the loop in his own lifeline. Now for Mo'Steel.

"Twenty."

Where was his friend's carabiner? "Turn a little, Mo!"

"I'm turning as fast as I can!"

"I mean your body. Turn this way!"

Jobs snatched the carabiner. It spun away, cartwheeling through space. A desperate lunge, a grab with clumsy gloved fingers.

"Ten seconds to burn."

He snagged the carabiner. *Snap!*

"Eight . . . seven . . ."

He lunged, drew Mo'Steel's lifeline up, and snapped the carabiner onto the handle.

"Six . . ."

Mo'Steel yelled, "What are you doing? I can't turn the thing if —"

Jobs pulled himself up, too fast, slammed his shoulder into the shuttle skin, spun outward, dangling in space.

Mo'Steel grabbed his arm, pulled him down, yanked the lifeline, and snapped it into place.

"Three . . ."

"See? Plenty of time," Mo'Steel said. "Two whole seconds to sit here and chat."

"One."

Less than twenty feet away, the orbiter's engines exploded into life. No smoke, no roiling cascade of superheated gas, just a jet as neat and symmetrical as a gas stove.

Jobs and Mo'Steel were slammed hard downward. Suddenly there was a downward. Suddenly there was weight as well as mass. Jobs was hanging by his waist, feeling like he weighed two tons. It was not the exorbitant acceleration of liftoff, but it still squeezed his lungs, bent him back, turned his spine into a letter *U*.

He was upside down, hanging head downward now, a tin can tied to a speeding car. The lifeline was extended fully, and stretching. The cone of fire was only a few feet below, blue-bright, weirdly silent.

Was he going to die? Was it now, his death?

He remembered the kid, the strange sleepwalking kid, Billy Weir. "You'll be there," he'd said to Jobs. "You'll be there."

Where? There.

The burn obscured a part of the planet turning beneath him. But the shuttle was rotating slightly at the same time, and now he could see the Rock.

"Mo! Are you okay?"

No answer. Maybe he hadn't keyed his mike. Maybe the burn was blanking out the signal. Or maybe Mo wasn't there to answer.

The acceleration seemed to go on forever. He had been hanging there, dangling helpless, straining for every breath forever.

And suddenly, all at once, it ended.

The cone of fire was gone. The acceleration

ceased. The ship was now moving at better than 25,000 miles per hour, but once again the sense of speed disappeared along with the sense of weight.

No death. Not yet.

"You boys still there?" Willett called.

"I'm okay," Jobs answered.

"Aaahhhh! Aaaahhhh!" Mo'Steel screamed into his mike.

"My friend is okay, too."

"Head for the airlock, you did good," the commander said.

Jobs moved hand-over-hand with ease up the length of the lifeline. Mo'Steel met him at the crank and they unhooked.

"Okay, that beat The Pipe," Mo'Steel said.

But Jobs didn't answer. He put his hand on his friend's shoulder and pointed.

Mo'Steel turned and the two of them hung there, suspended, side by side, as the Rock came to the end of its long trip.

CHAPTER TWENTY-THREE

"IT'S OVER."

Up close, so near Earth, the Rock looked very small. Seventy-six miles in diameter, it was nothing next to the planet measured in thousands of miles.

But, up close, so close, Jobs could see the speed of it. Against the backdrop of space you couldn't sense the awesome speed. But now, as it angled into the atmosphere, in the brief second in which it could be seen outlined against blue ocean, it seemed impossibly fast.

The Rock entered the atmosphere and for a flash became a spectacular special effect: The atmosphere burned, a red gash in its wake.

It struck the western edge of Portugal. Portugal and Spain were hit by a bullet the size of Connecticut. The Iberian peninsula was a trench, a ditch.

The Mediterranean Sea, trillions of gallons of water, exploded into steam. Every living thing in the water, every living thing ashore, was parboiled in an instant.

Portugal, Spain, southern France, all of Italy, the Balkans, the coast of northern Africa, Greece, southern Turkey, all the way to Israel was obliterated in less than five seconds. They were the cradles of Western civilization one second, a hell of super-heated steam and flying rock the next.

The destruction was too swift to believe. In the time Jobs could blink his eyes, Rome and Cairo, Athens and Barcelona, Istanbul and Jerusalem and Damascus were gone. Not reduced to rubble, not crushed, not devastated. This wasn't like war or any disaster humans understood. Rock became gravel, soil melted and fused, water was steam, living flesh was reduced to singed single cells. Nothing recognizable remained.

The impact explosion was a million nuclear bombs going off at once. The rock and soil and waters that had once defined a dozen nations formed a pillar of smoke and flying dirt and steam. The mushroom cloud punched up through the atmosphere, flinging dust and smoke particles clear into space.

Jobs could see a chunk of Earth, some fragment left half-intact, maybe twenty miles across, spin slowly up in the maelstrom. There were houses.

Buildings. A hint of tilled fields. Rising on the mushroom cloud, flying free, entering space itself.

The entire planet shuddered. It was possible to
see it from space: The ground rippled, as if rock and
soil were liquid. The shock wave was an earthquake
that toppled trees, collapsed every human-built
structure around the planet, caused entire mountain
chains to crumble.

The oceans rippled in tidal waves a thousand
feet high. The Atlantic Ocean rolled into New York
and over it, rolled into Charleston and over it, rolled
into Miami and washed across the entire state of
Florida. The ocean waters lapped against the Ap-
palachian Mountain chains, swamped everything in
their way, smothered all who had not been killed by
the blast or the shock wave.

People died having no idea why. People were
thrown from their beds, dashed against walls that
collapsed onto them. People who survived long
enough to find themselves buried alive beneath
green sea many miles deep.

Jobs saw the planet's rotation slow. The day
would stand still for the few who might still be alive.

The impact worked its damage on the fissures
and cracks in Earth's crust. Jobs watched the Atlantic Ocean split right down the middle, emptying

millions of cubic miles of water as if it was of no more consequence than pulling the plug on a bathroom sink.

The planet was breaking up. Cracking apart. Impossibly deep fissures raced at supersonic speeds around the planet. They cut through the crust, through the mantle, deeper than a thousand Grand Canyons.

Now the Pacific, too, drained away. It emptied into the molten core of Earth itself. The explosion dwarfed everything that had gone before. As Jobs watched, motionless, crying but not aware of it, Earth broke apart.

It was as if some invisible hand were ripping open an orange. A vast, irregular chunk of Earth separated slowly from the planet, spun sluggishly, slowly away. The sides of this moon-sized wedge scraped against the sides of the gash, gouged up countries, ground down mountains.

And now this wedge of Earth itself broke in half. Jobs saw what might have been California, his home, turn slowly toward the sun. *If anyone is left alive,* he thought, *if anyone is still alive, they'll see the sunrise this one last time.*

Earth lay still at last. Perhaps a quarter of the planet was bitten off, drifting away to form a second and a third Earth. The oceans were gone, boiled off into space. The sky was no longer blue but brown, as dirt and dust blotted out the sun. Here and there could still be seen patches of green. But it was impossible to believe, to hope, that any human being had survived.

All of humanity that still lived was aboard the shuttle that now slid slowly toward the distant sun.

The mike crackled to life. "Come on in, boys. It's over."

(CHAPTER TWENTY-FOUR)

"PUT ME TO SLEEP, OR KILL ME, BUT MAKE IT STOP."

In his berth Jobs swallowed the tube, forced it down into his stomach. The transparent lid closed over him. Sleep. Sleep. Death. What did it matter? How did you live when your world was dead?

He felt the drowsiness of hibernation. *Do it faster,* he thought, *put me to sleep, turn off my brain. Turn the lights out on the movie in my head, the pictures of all the faces, all the people I've known, the ones I liked and loved, the ones I cared nothing for, the ones I never knew.*

"Put me to sleep, or kill me, but make it stop," he whispered.

He was still awake to hear the distant, muffled explosion. A gun. Colonel Willett would not be coming along on this trip.

Sleep took Jobs. And Mo'Steel. The hibernation equipment slowed their hearts and then stopped them. Slowed the bouncing electrical impulses in their brains, and stopped them. They were as dead as the people of Earth, but with at least a hope of re-birth somewhere, sometime.

Tamara Hoyle was already deep in the hibernation death-sleep. But the technology had never been designed for pregnant women. The machine knew nothing of the fetus inside her.

2Face slept, her berth between those of her parents.

Yago slept, as alone now as ever.

D-Caf slept, calm at last.

Billy Weir lay unmoving, his body paralyzed. He could not hear. Could not see. Could not move. The hibernation equipment slowed every process, stopped every activity.

But Billy Weir did not sleep. His brain did not shut down.

The *Mayflower* fell toward the sun, accelerating all the while, faster and faster yet still painfully, piti-fully slow in the distances of space. It would fall toward the sun for years. And slowly come around the sun, for years. And gain still more speed and race away from the sun and past the shattered remains of dark Earth for years stretching into decades.

Centuries.

And still, Billy Weir would not sleep.

K.A. APPLEGATE

REMNANTS™

②

Destination Unknown

"IF THIS IS A DREAM, IT'S THE MOTHER, FATHER, SISTER, AND BROTHER OF WEIRD."

"You're alive," a voice said.

A hand shook Jobs's shoulder, but gently, seemingly knowing the pain he was in.

Slowly he revived. He saw a half-ruined face. A pretty girl, Asian, with half her face melted like wax.

"You probably don't remember me," she said. "I'm 2Face. We met back on Earth. Do you remember Earth? Do you remember what happened?"

He nodded dully. He looked, helpless to stop himself, at the filthy decay of his father's berth.

"A lot are like that," 2Face said. "I don't think very many of us are still alive. On my way up here I saw a few who looked alive. Sleeping, still. And there are some that . . . Some, I don't know."

Jobs searched her face. She looked as if she had been crying. But maybe that was because of the drooping eye on her burned side.

"Do you think you can walk?" 2Face asked.

"I don't know," Jobs said.

"I think maybe we should get out of here," 2Face said.

Jobs shook his head. "We have to help these . . ."

"We're too weak. I keep falling asleep. I just heard you, so I climbed up here. But we have to get out. Outside. This place is . . . there are dead people everywhere." Her voice that had been so calm was edging toward hysteria. "There's just things, people, stuff you don't, I mean, I was climbing up here because I heard you moving and I passed by . . . and my mom . . . it's just . . . and they don't even smell, you know, not like dead people, like nothing, or like, like yeast, like bread . . ."

"Take it easy, take it easy, don't think about it," Jobs said.

"Don't think about it?!" 2Face screamed. "Don't think about it?!"

Jobs grabbed her face in his hands. The melted flesh felt strange. She stared at him, wild.

"We start screaming we're never going to stop," Jobs said. "My brain is ready to explode, my mom and dad and everything. But we have to think. We have to think."

She nodded vigorously, searching his eyes as if looking for reflections of her own panic. "Okay, we stick together, okay?"

"Yeah," Jobs agreed readily. "We stick together. Help each other. Neither one of us thinks too much, okay? We just try and figure out . . ." He couldn't imagine what he had to figure out. The images of his parents, the fear that his little brother might awaken and see them for himself, all of it was too much, like he was trying to take a drink from a fire hose, too much data, too much horror.

2Face said, "Okay, come on, we stick together." Her calm had returned, almost as if it was her turn to be rational while he fought the torrent of fear and grief. "Okay, we need to find out what happened. Are we . . . I mean, where are we, the ship I mean? Did we land somewhere? Are we still in space?"

"Yeah. Yeah," Jobs nodded, anxious to come to grips with simple problems. "Yeah. We're not weightless. Okay. We're not weightless. So we can't be in space. Unless we're accelerating. Then we'd have weight."

"That's good, think about that," 2Face said.

"Let's go up. To the bridge. We can see where we are."

"To the bridge. Maybe the captain is up there, he can tell us, if he made it I mean."

"He didn't," Jobs said, remembering a dull thump, the sound of a gun being fired. The sound of a man's choice not to live on when his wife and children and home and very species were gone. "Long story. There were some problems. Come on. Let's go to the bridge."

Each step up the ladder was painful. But each step was less painful than the step before.

They climbed past the place where D-Caf and his brother, Mark Melman, had stowed away. Where Mark had shot the Marine sergeant. What was her name? Jobs couldn't remember. Had she survived? How could she, she'd been shot, badly wounded when they bundled her into a hibernation berth. His own perfectly healthy parents had not survived, how could a wounded woman?

And Mo'Steel. What about Mo? He should check on Mo.

No. No more hideous plexiglass coffins. He didn't want to see any more horrors.

They reached the crawlway that connected the

cargo area to the flight deck. The hatch was open. Jobs went in first.

He had to climb up. The tunnel was meant to be used either in a weightless environment or crawled through when the shuttle was at rest horizontally.

The tunnel opened onto a space below the flight deck. It was mostly crammed with lockers. What they contained he didn't know, but water would have been his first choice. He was desperately thirsty.

There was a ladder that in this position was more an impediment than a help. He crawled onto the flight deck. It was designed for horizontal flight, with the seats set in such a way that during the landing phase, the pilots would be positioned like the pilots of any commercial jet. So when Jobs entered the flight deck the seats were above him, over his back.

He stood up and stretched.

Looking straight up Jobs could see a sliver of light through the small cockpit windshield. Like looking up through a skylight. Strange. The sky was blue, and for a moment he felt a leap of irrational hope. They were home! On Earth. All of it a dream.

But the blue of the sky was not the depthless, indeterminate blue of earth's sky. The sky seemed to be made up of blue scales. Dabs of blue and dabs of violet. Even streaks of green. And the cloud he saw was no cloud that had ever floated through Earth's sky. It was white in parts, but also brown, with streaks of brown dragged across the white.

The whole mass of the sky moved, vibrated. As if the wind blew, but blew nowhere in particular, just reshuffled the scales and smears of color.

"What is it?" 2Face asked. She was staring up past him.

"I don't know."

He helped her to her feet. They stood on what would normally be a vertical bulkhead.

The shuttle had landed. Somewhere. Gravity was downward, which meant that, impossible as it clearly was, it had landed nose up. It had landed in take-off position. Utterly impossible.

The shuttle had no way to achieve this. The thought had been that the ship's computers would, on sensing the right circumstances, trim the solar sails to achieve deceleration and enter orbit around some theoretical, hoped for, prayed for planet.

After that, the thinking was that any orbit would inevitably deteriorate, and the shuttle would then be able to land in its normal configuration under the guidance of a revived pilot.

Of course, the shuttle landed on a smooth, paved runway. Not on prairie. Not on water. Not on mountainsides. Not in craters.

Jobs knew (just as everyone aboard knew) what a mishmash of faint hopes and ludicrous delusions this mission represented. There never had been anything more than a disappearingly small chance of success.

Fly through space toward no particular goal, have the solar sails work both to accelerate and decelerate and then have the absurd good luck to land on a planet with reasonable gravity and a very convenient landing strip positioned wherever they happened to touch down?

Absurd.

But to do all that and somehow end up vertical?

"Maybe we're still asleep," Jobs muttered.

"I don't think so, Duck. I don't have dreams like this."

The voice was instantly familiar.

"Mo?"

Mo'Steel leaned out into view overhead. He was perched in the captain's seat. He was smiling, but nothing like his usual Labrador retriever grin.

"I'm alive," Mo'Steel reported. "If this is a dream, it's the mother, father, sister, and brother of weird. We got all of weird's cousins in on this. Come on up. You gotta see this. You have *got* to see this."

Light-Years From Home...And On Their Own

BGA 0-590-87997-9	Remnants	#1: The Mayflower Project	$4.99 US
BGA 0-590-88074-8	Remnants	#2: Destination Unknown	$4.99 US
BGA 0-590-88078-0	Remnants	#3: Them	$4.99 US
BGA 0-590-88193-0	Remnants	#4: Nowhere Land	$4.99 US
BGA 0-590-88194-9	Remnants	#5: Mutation	$4.99 US
BGA 0-590-88195-7	Remnants	#6: Breakdown	$4.99 US
BGA 0-590-88196-5	Remnants	#7: Isolation	$4.99 US
BGA 0-590-88273-2	Remnants	#8: Mother, May I?	$4.99 US
BGA 0-590-88492-1	Remnants	#9: No Place Like Home	$4.99 US
BGA 0-590-88494-8	Remnants	#10: Lost and Found	$4.99 US
BGA 0-590-88495-6	Remnants	#11: Dream Storm	$4.99 US
BGA 0-590-88522-7	Remnants	#12: Aftermath	$4.99 US

Available wherever you buy books, or use this order form.

Continue the exciting journey online at **www.scholastic.com/remnants**

A key to a house no one can see...
seven days to unlock a mystery.

GARTH NIX

keys to the kingdom

Arthur was supposed to die, until a
mysterious visitor brought him a very
strange key that opens a house that only
he can see. Arthur doesn't know what's
inside the house. But he knows that his
life and the lives of countless others
depend on his finding out. Once through
the door, his adventure begins—an
adventure that will put him to
the ultimate test.

Coming
in June

www.scholastic.com/books

Available wherever books are sold.